MARRIED
FOR THE
ITALIAN'S HEIR

BY
RACHAEL THOMAS

MILLS
BOON

All rights reserved including the right of reproduction in whole
or in part in any form. This edition is published by arrangement with
Harlequin Books S.A.

This is a work of fiction. Names, characters, places, locations and
incidents are purely fictional and bear no relationship to any real
life individuals, living or dead, or to any actual places, business
establishments, locations, events or incidents. Any resemblance is
entirely coincidental.

This book is sold subject to the condition that it shall not, by way of
trade or otherwise, be lent, resold, hired out or otherwise be circulated
without the prior consent of the publisher in any form of binding or
cover other than that in which it is published and without a similar
condition including this condition being imposed on the subsequent
purchaser.

® and ™ are trademarks owned and used by the trademark owner
and/or its licensee. Trademarks marked with ® are registered with the
United Kingdom Patent Office and/or the Office for Harmonisation in
the Internal Market and in other countries.

First Published in Great Britain 2016
By Mills & Boon, an imprint of HarperCollins*Publishers*
1 London Bridge Street, London, SE1 9GF

© 2016 Harlequin Books S.A.

MORAY COUNCIL LIBRARIES & INFO.SERVICES	
20 41 49 43	
Askews & Holts	
RF	

Special thanks and acknowledgement go to Rachael Thomas
for her contribution to the Brides for Billionaires series.

ISBN: 978-0-263-91661-4

Our policy is to use papers that are natural, renewable and recyclable
products and made from wood grown in sustainable forests. The logging
and manufacturing processes conform to the legal environmental
regulations of the country of origin.

Printed and bound in Spain
by CPI, Barcelona

Rachael Thomas has always loved reading romance, and is thrilled to be a Mills & Boon author. She lives and works on a farm in Wales—a far cry from the glamour of a Modern Romance story—but that makes slipping into her characters' worlds all the more appealing. When she's not writing or working on the farm she enjoys photography and visiting historical castles and grand houses. Visit her at rachaelthomas.co.uk.

Books by Rachael Thomas

Mills & Boon Modern Romance

The Sheikh's Last Mistress
New Year at the Boss's Bidding
From One Night to Wife
Craving Her Enemy's Touch
Claimed by the Sheikh
A Deal Before the Altar

The Billionaire's Legacy

To Blackmail a Di Sione

Visit the Author Profile page at
millsandboon.co.uk for more titles.

For Mum

PROLOGUE

Two months ago

PIPER LOST ALL sense of reason as his kiss seared her skin and his accomplished touch brought her body to life in a way she'd never known. The pain and grief that this day held for her were blotted out as he whispered words of Italian that sounded romantic, but she had no hope of understanding them.

She gloried in his embrace, for the first time in many months feeling treasured, wanted and needed. What would come after this moment she couldn't think about now. She didn't want to face the emptiness. All she wanted was to abandon herself to this man and his passion, to yield to his kisses and give herself utterly and completely to the moment—and to him.

She gasped in frustration as he stopped kissing her. He pulled away and looked down at her, his sinfully dark caramel eyes full of desire—for *her*. Empowered by this, she smiled at him, unable to hide the longing that was tearing through her faster than lightning. She'd never been desired by any man, and had certainly never been kissed the way he had just kissed her. But, more than that, it was the way she wanted him to kiss her again and again.

This man was a skilled lover, and the way he was looking at her now, with raw lust that vibrated through the semi-darkness of the hotel room, she knew there was no turning back—not that she wanted to. The attraction between them had been too fierce, too strong, even before he'd suggested they leave the party.

Tonight she would give herself to this man. But she was well aware there wouldn't be a tomorrow. She might be an innocent woman discovering the pleasure of a man's touch, but she knew not to expect more. She'd worked as a waitress at many society parties in Sydney and in London and she had recognised him as a playboy—a man who wanted one uncommitted night of passion, who loved and left women. Tonight she didn't care about her dream to settle down with the right man. Tonight she wanted the wrong man.

She wanted to drown her sorrow in the passion even she couldn't deny, which had ignited between them from the very first moment their eyes had met as he'd arrived at the party. It had arced between them as if they were meant to be here together, caught up in a moment of passion which would surely change her…change her life. How, she didn't know. She just knew that this moment was one she had to explore.

He touched her face, tracing the pad of his thumb down her cheek, and she closed her eyes as her knees threatened to give way. He pulled her closer, holding her tightly with one arm, keeping her body pressed against the hardness of his, making her virginal body pulse so wildly with unquenched desire it was as if the conclusion of the kiss was already sealed. As was her fate.

'Before we go any further, do we need protection?' His husky and heavily accented voice shimmered over her, and her senses were so confused by the desire which burned through her Piper couldn't think straight.

'Protection?' The whispered word sounded so seductive she could hardly believe it was *her* voice. How had the sensible and shy woman she usually was become such a seductress?

'I intend to make love to you, *cara.*'

He slipped off his suit jacket in a purposeful way which made her heart race as much as his words did. All sensible thought vanished from her as she watched him turn and toss it onto a nearby chair. His white shirt was bright in the partial darkness of the room.

She quivered with anticipation as he stepped back to her, excited and terrified about what would happen next. With deliberate slowness he took her in his arms again and kissed her. Then his hand moved down her neck and along her shoulder, slipping under the strap of her dress, sliding it away. As his lips followed the blazing trail of his hand she let her head fall back and gave herself up to the abandonment of the moment.

'Sorted…' She gasped the word as his kisses moved down her neck, hardly able to think straight because of the fire each kiss ignited within her.

'Then there is nothing to stop us.'

With unnerving ease he pulled the zip at the side of her dress and the black silk slithered down her body. The heat of embarrassment rushed over her, and she watched his face as he touched her breast, his fingers concentrating on the hardened peak of her nipple, making her gasp with pleasure. Then he lowered his head and teased the other nipple with his tongue until she thought she might explode with pleasure.

'That is so…' She closed her eyes as heat seared within her, unable to say anything else.

'Do you want me, *cara*?'

His warm breath increased the sensation of delirium as his tongue teased her nipple.

'I want you...' She struggled to say the words as he continued to work his magic. She entwined her fingers in his thick hair, not wanting him ever to stop. 'To make love to me.'

He laughed softly against her breast, the sensation making her writhe against him.

'I can think of nothing better, you little tease.'

His accent thrilled her as much as his words, intensifying this new and exciting need inside her, pushing the real Piper further away.

'Now.' She pulled him close against her, wanting to feel his body, to taste his skin. 'I want you *now*.'

A soft, sexy laugh escaped him and he let go of her briefly, putting her at arm's length. The black silk of her dress slithered to the floor in a pool around her feet, leaving her in skimpy black panties and strappy sandals.

His dark gaze roved over her near nakedness and the air between them sparked with desire. A flash of her usual shyness threatened, but she pushed it back, refusing to allow it into this moment, and reached for him. Her need to see more of him and touch him made her pull so hard at his shirt buttons they popped off.

His feral growl of pleasure pushed her on, making her want him, want *this* even more. She couldn't stop now—couldn't be her usual cautious self and spend the rest of her life wondering *What if?* Tonight she would experience 'What if?' She couldn't let this moment go by without responding to it.

In a movement so swift, so decisive, he pushed her back onto the bed, pulling off his white shirt and exposing his muscled torso, dusted in dark hair. Then, with a wicked gleam in those devil-may-care eyes, he removed every last scrap of clothing from his glorious body.

She watched, entranced and excited, as he stepped towards her, towering over her. She trembled in anticipation as she lay there, his gaze never leaving hers. Her heart pounded so hard she was sure the whole of London could hear it, and a sigh of pleasure escaped her as he lowered himself over her, the hardness of his arousal almost too much.

He spoke again in Italian as he kissed down her throat and she ran her hands over his strong back, pressing her nails into his skin. But still it wasn't enough. Still she wanted more.

Driven by a powerful need she no longer had any control over, she slipped her hands between their bodies and he lifted himself slightly, allowing her to touch him. She wanted to feel him, to torment him as he'd done her. But still it wasn't enough. She wanted to remove the last barriers of clothing and feel him touch her intimately before possessing her completely.

Urgency took over and she clung to him, raising her hips, her body begging his for release and the oblivion of passion. She wanted him so much. It was as if she'd been waiting for this moment—for him.

'*Dio mio*. You are a goddess sent to torment me.'

His guttural voice together with his insistent kisses up her neck was almost too much, and she knew that it had to be now—that they had to come together, that there was no turning back.

He moved, clasping his hands around her wrists and pinning her arms either side of her head. The wild look in his eyes was as terrifying as it was exciting. His breath was coming hard and fast as he fixed her with those dark, sexy eyes. She lifted her hips, clasping her legs around him as her need to be one with him increased.

Another curse left his lips and he let one of her arms go as he raised his hips and ripped her black panties from her. Her shocked gasp only encouraged him further, and he barely paused as she pressed her nakedness against him, feeling the heat of his erection intimately.

'*Per Dio.*'

The words rushed from him as she moved, bringing them together. He thrust into her, her startled cry making him stop. She glanced up to see a furious frown on his handsome face, but she couldn't let it end there. She wanted total possession. She wanted him to take her, make her his. Even if it was only for tonight.

'Don't stop.' She lifted her hips, taking him deeper inside her as she raised her head and pressed kisses against his chest, tasting the salty tang of desire on his skin.

'You're a…' he whispered hoarsely.

But she pressed her lips against his, hiding the truth as she used the unrelenting need in her body and lifted herself up to him, making his possession deep and powerful, forcing him to surrender to the moment too.

Another feral curse left him as he joined her in the frenzied dance of sex. It was so exquisite, so much more than she'd ever dared to hope it could be, that as she hovered on the brink of oblivion she cried out, holding him tight against her as several tears escaped, sliding down her face. She buried her face against his chest, inhaling the sexy scent of him, knowing it would be etched in her memory for ever.

As would the moment she'd lost her virginity, becoming a real woman with a man whose name she didn't even know.

As her heart rate slowed and his body relaxed she moved, but he caught an arm around her, pulling her close against him. 'You are not going anywhere yet, *cara*.'

Those sultry words made her mind spin—as did the reality of what she'd done. Through the fog of desire rational thought was finally becoming clear. She'd lost her virginity and jeopardised her new job—all for a man who hadn't even bothered with the pleasantries of an introduction. His kisses and soft words had seduced her on a day when she was at her most vulnerable, a day when she needed to know she was alive, prove she could be a woman in charge of her life.

His breathing deepened as he slept, and even though her body was held tightly against his Piper knew she had no option but to leave. She might have experienced the most wonderful night, but this wasn't who she was.

She slipped carefully from the bed and quietly gathered her clothes, dressing in the near darkness. He stirred and she looked at him—at his handsome face, his lean body partially covered by the white sheet—committing it all to her memory, because this was a man who didn't want anything other than casual affairs. Despite her naivety, she knew this.

Quietly she left the room of the man whose name she didn't even know—the man she would never see again as she returned to being the shy woman who'd arrived in London from Australia only a year before.

CHAPTER ONE

FURIOUS AT THE way his life had begun to unravel over the last two weeks, Dante Mancini pushed back the effects of too much whisky at last night's impromptu meeting. He tried not to think of the outrageous solution Benjamin Carter had proposed to counteract the damning article *Celebrity Spy!* had run.

The scandalous piece—naming himself, Ben Carter, Sheikh Zayn Al-Ghamdi and Xander Trakas as the world's most debauched bachelors—had done untold damage to their favourite charity, The Hope Foundation. Now those who ran it had demanded they clean up their acts or step aside as patrons. To make matters worse, a business deal he'd been working on was in danger of collapsing because of the damage to his reputation—he was a bachelor who played the field and now everyone knew it.

Could Ben's idea work? Would taking such drastic action as marriage divert unwanted attention from the charity *and* secure his most lucrative business deal yet? Possibly. But was he prepared to take the gamble...?

Dante pushed open the door to his office building, not bothering to remove his sunglasses and definitely not ready to admit that the copious amount of whisky he'd drunk whilst being told he needed to find himself a wife was the reason for his fierce headache and foul mood.

He stabbed at the button to call the elevator and inhaled deeply as he waited, still fuming that Bettino D'Antonio was pulling out of the deal because he, Dante Mancini, and his company didn't uphold family values.

As the doors to the elevator swished open he walked in, desperate for a moment of solitude before he entered the suite of offices which served as the headquarters for his self-built global business empire dealing in renewable energies. In a bid to bring back some control and chase away the threatening headache he inhaled deeply once again.

The doors closed and instantly his senses were on alert. His memory rushed back to an illicit night of hot sex in a London hotel with an unknown redhead who'd haunted his dreams and stalked his thoughts each day ever since.

She had been wild and passionate, and yet as he'd made her his he'd realised she was a virgin. A fluid curse left him as the elevator doors closed, trapping him inside with a memory which only added to his unaccustomed bad mood. It irritated the hell out of him that those gorgeous green eyes continued to haunt him and that, despite the alcohol still in his system from last night, his blood heated at the memory and a shot of lust hurtled round him.

'Maledizione.' He *never* thought of a woman once their affair was over, and the redhead encounter had been two months ago. Well and truly over.

He clenched his hands into tight fists at his sides. Now was *not* the time to become embroiled in memories of one meaningless night. He had to remain in control—focus on the matter in hand. He couldn't allow that piece of gossip in *Celebrity Spy!* to jeopardise one of the biggest deals he'd ever gone after, or to tarnish the work of the charity he helped to fund. But neither was he about to be dictated to by Benjamin Carter. He had absolutely no desire to settle down in that very elusive state of marital bliss just to salvage his reputation. There had to be another way and he'd find it—of that he was sure.

Not a moment too soon the elevator doors opened and he left the memory-evoking scent of perfume and marched into his office. His head thumped mercilessly from last night's excess of whisky and his temper was frayed from the latest developments on the deal.

His secretary jumped up eagerly as he stormed in but he refused to indulge in his usual morning pleasantries. He didn't have the stamina for niceties right now. All he wanted was total silence and coffee—strong and black.

'I don't want to be disturbed.' He snapped the instruction at her as he strode past her desk, desperate for the solitude of his office with its sought-after views over the old quarter of Rome.

'Signor Mancini…' she began, overriding his instruction, and he stopped and looked at her, about to open his office door, glad of the sunglasses he still wore.

The last thing he wanted his secretary to know was that he was suffering from an uncharacteristic over-indulgence of alcohol. After his meeting with Ben and the others he'd managed to catch an hour or two of sleep during the overnight flight back to Rome on his private jet, but that hadn't helped dull the effects of the whisky. All he needed was to be left alone.

'No calls. No meetings. Nothing.' He threw the words at her and as she took a breath to protest turned from her and burst into his office. He slammed the door and closed his eyes, taking a deep breath. The world had gone mad. Everything he'd worked so hard to achieve seemed in danger of falling to pieces around him.

He muttered a curse and strode across his large office, pressed the button on his coffee machine, then stood at the windows looking out over the city that had at first been a hard and demanding mistress but was now one of only two places in the world where he felt completely at ease.

As the welcome aroma of coffee filled his office he heard movement behind him and tensed. He turned slowly to see just who it was in his office, aware now that his secretary's unusual insistence on speaking to him must have been to warn him that he had someone waiting for him.

What he *didn't* expect to see was the flame-haired siren who'd haunted him since that night two months ago, when she'd slipped from his bed in the early hours, long before he'd woken. *Not* something he was accustomed to.

'I hope you don't mind that I waited in here for you…' The redhead's soft voice wavered with uncertainty and, dressed in jeans and a navy knitted poncho, she certainly didn't resemble the glamorous self-assured beauty he'd bedded that night. But then she hadn't been all she'd pretended to be that night, had she? She hadn't been an experienced seductress. She'd been a virgin. A fact she'd kept from him until it had been too late.

He pulled off his sunglasses and looked at her. How had she found him? How did she know who he was? Those few hours in his hotel room had been so passionate, so filled with lustful need that they hadn't even exchanged names, let alone phone numbers.

Icy-cold fingers of dread clutched at him. Was she

here to use that story in *Celebrity Spy!* for some kind of blackmail? Did she want to sell a kiss-and-tell story? Was that why she'd come to Rome unannounced? To demand money from him for her silence?

'As a matter of fact I do.' The angry bitterness in his voice barely concealed his disappointment at this realisation. He'd placed her on some kind of pedestal since that night, his thoughts constantly returning to her like a lovesick teenager. She'd got to him in a way no other woman had come close to doing. Even now his blood heated at the knowledge that she was so close, just as it had when he'd smelt the lingering trace of what he now knew to be her perfume in the elevator moments ago.

She stood up and he let his gaze travel quickly down her jean-clad legs, remembering how they'd felt as she'd wrapped them around him. Savagely he dragged his mind back to the present. Dwelling on one night of sex was not in his nature.

'What do you want?' He fired the question at her.

'I just have one thing I need to say and then I will go.'

Her voice still held uncertainty and her face looked pale. Was that just because she wore hardly any make-up?

She looked totally different from the seductress who'd tempted him from the party that night, and she stood before him now looking every bit the innocent and inexperienced virgin she had been when he'd taken her to his hotel room. But she wasn't a virgin any longer. He had been her first lover and he wanted to know why she had kept that from him. The question wouldn't come. As she looked at him he sensed something much bigger, much more threatening.

'How much?' he demanded, narrowing his eyes as he tried to gauge her reaction, angry that he'd put himself in this position, that he hadn't exercised his usual caution where women were concerned.

Her delicate brows flew together. 'How much what?'

He stepped closer and the scent of her perfume teased at his memory again. He closed his mind to the images which threatened to engulf him. The woman who stood before him now was very different from the woman who'd teased him until he'd all but lost his mind as well as his control.

He sighed and walked towards his desk, tossing his sunglasses down before leaning on its solid wood, fixing her with a hard glare. 'How much do you want? For your silence?'

'I'm not about to tell the world,' she snapped back at him, her voice full of injustice.

He only just managed to stifle a smile. The fiery redhead had briefly surfaced from behind the façade of unassuming inexperience she had adopted.

'Then why are you here, *cara*? And, more to the point, how did you find me?' Already he was bored with this conversation. His head thumped cruelly and he wanted nothing more than to sit down in silence. He had a deal to salvage and he didn't need Little Miss Shy adding to the mix of hurdles he had to power over.

'There was an article…' she said softly as he walked back towards the windows.

He turned to face her and noticed how she followed his every move, turning herself slightly to maintain eye contact with him. It made him suspicious.

'I'm more than aware that there was an article,' he growled back at her, the tension in his head reaching almost breaking point. This tedious conversation should have ended when she'd named her price—right before he threw her out. So why hadn't she? More to the point, why hadn't he thrown her out?

'That is how I got your name.' He raised his brows as she blushed before continuing. 'We didn't exactly have time to exchange details.'

Exchanging details had been the last thing on his mind. All he'd wanted was her naked and beneath him. He'd been rash and uncontrolled. Hell, he'd even taken her word that she was on the pill. Something he'd *never* succumbed to, no matter how deliciously tempting the woman.

'True, but we had much more fun that way, did we not, *cara*?' He smiled at her, allowing himself to remember her eagerness, her insistence which had so turned him on, testing his control beyond its usual limits.

'Piper.' Her eyes narrowed as she glared at him, the green depths of them sparking wildly.

'Piper?' he repeated, his mind still not able to function as it should. Hell, he hadn't even had an espresso yet to banish the remnants of whisky, even though the welcome aroma now filled the office.

'My name is Piper. Piper Riley.'

He nodded. 'And now that we are both in possession of each other's names, perhaps you'd tell me exactly why you are here.' Once again he moved across his office and glanced at the woman who'd been just the redhead in his mind until today. As before, she moved to face him. Now she had a name would she continue to linger in his mind so temptingly? He hoped not.

'I needed to see you because...' She faltered and he folded his arms across his chest, becoming increasingly irritated by the conversation.

'*Dio mio*. Just say what you have to say and leave. I don't have time for games.'

'Very well.' She stood taller, lifted her chin a fraction and looked directly at him. 'I'm pregnant.'

Dante had thought the previous twenty-four hours had been filled with nothing but trouble, swallowing up his usual cavalier attitude. He had never expected—or wanted—those words to be said to him. He couldn't be a father—not when he'd already proved his inability to look after anyone.

'How?'

The word shot from him before he had time to think, time to compose himself, but she stood resolutely before him. Even the heated redness which rushed over her pale face for a second time didn't alter the fact that she had suddenly become bolder and more confident— much more like the woman he'd made love to that night.

Piper held her ground, remaining rigidly still, focusing her full attention on the man whose baby she was carrying. A man whose reputation had been plastered all over the tabloids in recent weeks, one of the world's most eligible and debauched bachelors. He was far from ideal father material, but she couldn't deny him the knowledge that he was going to be a father—much less deny her child the right to a father.

She watched him as he prowled around his office, oblivious to the fact that the coffee he evidently needed was ready. He looked as immaculately stylish as he had the night of the party. The only difference was the hint of stubbly shadow at his jaw and the lines of tension on his face, which stirred her sympathy. But she couldn't let sentiment get in the way. Not now she knew exactly who she was dealing with.

'I think we both know how.'

She couldn't believe the seductive purr which wrapped around those words as she looked at him, wondering just what kind of effect this man still had on her. Her heart raced wildly and her stomach somersaulted. She wasn't at all convinced it was just her nerves at the situation. It was the darkly passionate man she'd lost her virginity to—Dante Mancini. A playboy and exceedingly proud of it, if the article she'd stumbled across in *Celebrity Spy!* was to be believed.

'What I mean is how, when you allowed me to believe that the protection I wanted to use wasn't necessary?' His words were slow and his accent heavy, as if he couldn't take in what she'd told him—or the implications.

Yes, that was the question she'd asked herself as she'd done the first pregnancy test—and the second. It had changed to the question of how she could have been so stupid as she'd done a third, and by the time she'd torn the packaging from the fourth and final test it had changed to words she never usually used, followed by panic at what she was going to do.

Being a single mother was *not* what she wanted. She'd grown up with a doting father and had always wanted that for her children. And now she was pregnant with this man's baby.

'In case you weren't aware, I had never been in such a situation with a man before. I assumed when you mentioned protection that it had been dealt with.' She hurled the words at him, furious at herself but even angrier that he'd balked at taking such responsibility.

He walked towards her, suspicion in his dark eyes, and she fought hard against the memory of them being full of desire for her, full of need for her and overflowing with passion. It had been a moment out of time that she'd wanted to remember for ever. Now, thanks to the legacy of that night, she had no choice.

'And how do I know you didn't go straight from my bed to that of another man? How do I know the baby you claim to carry is mine?'

She gasped in shock at his fiercely cold words. She'd played out many scenarios in her head over recent weeks, but none had been as brutally attacking as this. In a spur-of-the-moment decision she'd booked a ticket to Rome, because all she'd wanted to do was tell him, face to face, that he was going to be a father. She'd never anticipated anything more. The close bond she'd had with her father had made it impossible for her to do anything else but tell Dante Mancini personally. She'd foolishly believed that he'd want to know that those wonderfully passionate few hours together had created a new life. His child.

How wrong she'd been.

Defeat washed over her, followed by tiredness. She hadn't even booked a hotel. Once she'd made up her mind all she'd wanted was to get to Rome as soon as possible and to do what she considered the right thing before her confidence deserted her.

'There are tests that can determine such things.' She ploughed her fingers into her hair, pulling it off her face, holding it before letting it fall back. She was too tired to deal with this now. She'd felt sick for the duration of the flight, going over and over how to tell him. Trying to second-guess his reaction.

'Then there will be a test carried out as soon as it is safe to do so.'

The harsh words focused her mind acutely.

'I have no intention of taking your word for such a claim.'

'In that case you may be interested to know it can be done in a few weeks' time.' She couldn't help the rush of triumph as he glared at her. Had he expected her to flounder, to back away and leave without fighting her corner—her child's corner? As the battle of what to do had waged in her mind she'd done her research on the internet, and she knew that, within two weeks if he demanded it, she could confirm that he was the father.

He moved towards her—so close that she could see the flecks of black in the caramel-brown of his eyes, almost obliterating their colour. She could also detect the faint hint of alcohol and wondered if he had left another woman's bed that morning, after a night of sex and champagne like the one *they'd* shared. The thought sickened her and nausea rushed over her again. Her knees threatened to buckle as the reality of her shattered and foolish dreams sank in.

'You sound very convinced that the child is mine.'

He sounded indifferent to her distress, his accent intensified, and being so close to him brought back memories of their night together, increasing the almost overwhelming nausea. She gathered herself quickly. She couldn't break down now. Not here. Not in front of him.

'You are the only man I have ever slept with. That night we spent together was totally out of character for me.' She pushed down her reasons for acting on the undeniable attraction which had sparked so outrageously to life between them. She'd tried to continue working, but with his hot gaze all but stripping her naked right there in the middle of the party it had been almost impossible.

'So why did you do it?'

He walked slowly round her and she turned, needing to keep him firmly in her line of vision, and inwardly she cursed the lack of sight in her left eye that she'd been born with. She wanted to tell him to stand still, but she hated people knowing, and thanks to the operation she'd had as a child and the contact lenses she wore there wasn't any need to explain endlessly any more.

She took a deep breath. Honesty was the best way, and if he wanted to know why she'd gone hand in hand with him to his hotel room she would tell him. 'It was the first anniversary of my father's death, and I guess I wasn't my normal self.'

His penetrating gaze slid down her body and she swallowed down the nerves that were threatening to get the better of her. 'And is *this* your normal self?'

'Yes,' she snapped, hurt by his scathing tone.

She knew she looked nothing like the woman he'd taken to his hotel room. Not only that, she knew she was far from the self-assured woman who'd carried out her job dressed up to the nines in borrowed clothes and fresh out of the beauty salon. That woman had been so far removed from who she really was it was almost laughable—except Dante Mancini didn't look the least bit amused.

'*Va bene.* That can easily be sorted.' He reached towards her and pushed her hair back from her face so gently it might almost have been an intimate and loving gesture—*almost*.

Shocked by the heat of his fingers as they grazed her face, she stepped back. 'What do you mean, that can easily be sorted?'

'The woman I met in London exists. She was very real as she smiled at me, enticing me with her beautiful green eyes. She was also very real as I undressed her, kissed her and made love to her.'

She bit down on the urge to tell him that woman had never really existed. That night she'd been someone else, driven by the need for physical contact and the spark of sexual attraction which had exploded as they'd first made eye contact. Since that night she'd lost her job because of her dalliance with a client and discovered that she was pregnant. The woman he remembered would never be able to exist again. Already she'd changed.

'That may be so, but I have no intention of being that woman again. All I came here to achieve was making you aware of the fact that you are to be a father.' Inwardly she cursed her impulsiveness at coming to Rome. What had she been thinking? That love and happiness would follow?

'And now that I *am* aware we will do things my way.'

He strode back to the windows and stood looking out over Rome as the early winter sunshine danced on the rooftops of a city she'd always longed to visit.

'We will do no such thing.' Again she questioned her motives for being here. 'I want nothing. You can go back to your wild lover-boy existence. Goodbye, Dante.'

She took a deep breath as he squared his shoulders against her verbal attack, then walked briskly to the door of his office. All she wanted was to escape. To run away and hide so she could nurse her wounds and rebuild her damaged dreams of a happy-ever-after. How stupid she'd been to harbour any hope that he would stand by her, take on the role of father. What she'd read in *Celebrity Spy!* should have been enough to extinguish those hopes long before she'd boarded the plane.

She heard his curse before she saw him as he put

himself between her and the door, and she wondered if he'd guessed she couldn't see him from her left side— or anything else, for that matter. Was he exploiting the weakness she took such great pains to conceal?

'Let me pass,' she demanded as anger and disappointment collided inside her, making her voice sharp and fierce.

'You are not going anywhere. We have things to discuss, things to settle.'

'Such as?' She folded her arms beneath the knitted poncho she'd opted for early this morning as she'd left her small flat in London.

Dante looked at Piper and fought the urge to step back and let her go. He knew she was capable of walking away with something he'd never wanted—a child. But his business mind had worked overtime as she'd spat fury and fire at him. Piper carried his child—the one thing that might now be the answer to all the problems which had erupted since that damn article.

'My child.'

He couldn't and wouldn't think any further about the plan that had formulated in his mind.

'The one you tried hard to deny could even *be* yours until I mentioned the paternity test?'

The accusation in her voice cut deep, touching a part of him he hadn't known existed.

'You are carrying my child, my heir, and no matter how that has come about I will support you. Of that there is no question.' Outwardly he was in control…inwardly his past mistakes rushed at him. But he couldn't turn his back on his flesh and blood. He might have got it wrong in the past, but this was his child. 'But naturally there will be conditions attached.'

'I don't want your grudging support, Dante. I want more than that from you for my child—or nothing at all.'

The indignation in her voice reverberated around the office and her green eyes looked so fierce he actually wanted to kiss her. To feel her lips against his once more and kiss away all that fury, replacing it with the passion he knew only too well existed within her.

'I don't care what you say you want. You wouldn't have come all this way to tell me you are carrying my child if you didn't want *something*, Piper.' He liked the feel of her name on his tongue, but still suspicion niggled at him. 'Perhaps I was right the first time. Is it money that will buy your silence?'

Her green eyes blazed with fury and anger emanated from her in palpable waves. 'I want no such thing, and I can see I have made a very big mistake in thinking you would be even remotely interested in our baby.'

She turned and grabbed the door handle, pulling the door open, but his reactions were quick and he pressed his palm against the door, slamming it shut before she'd even opened it wide enough to walk through.

'You are not going anywhere until this is sorted, *mia cara*.' He leant close to her left ear and whispered his warning, surprised when she jumped away, turning to glare once more at him. The threat in his voice had made her look vulnerable, and his proximity made her as nervous as a kitten, but still she pulled herself together and prepared to fight.

'I am not your *mia cara*.' She all but spat the words at him, like a wild cat which had been cornered. 'And I want nothing from you. Forget you ever saw me.'

How could he forget her when ever since that night in London she'd been in his thoughts? An unnamed lover who'd given him her virginity and a night he would never forget.

Benjamin Carter's suggestion floated once again on the periphery of his thoughts. Piper's arrival at his office couldn't have been more perfectly timed. Her news—unwelcome at any other time—fitted perfectly into his rapidly forming plan. He needed a wife and she carried his child.

'That will not happen—not when you are carrying my child.' He held her arms gently, preventing any further attempts to flee. 'Marriage is the only option.'

CHAPTER TWO

'MARRIAGE?' THE WORD spluttered from Piper and she blinked at Dante, acutely aware of his hands holding her and scorching her skin through the layers she wore, setting free memories she'd rather not deal with right at this moment.

'If you didn't come here for money then it must be for a ring on your finger.'

The callous tones of his accented voice were splintered with bitterness, shattering any faint and futile hopes that what they'd shared in London might have been the start of something. That his rash proposal was for real.

Who was she trying to fool? She had been nothing more than an amusing diversion from a dull dinner party. And wasn't that precisely why she'd slipped from his bed in the early hours, stealing a last lingering glance at him as he'd slept? She'd hoped to save her job and her reputation by leaving before the hotel had come to life, but even that attempt had been in vain.

'Have you *any* idea how arrogant you sound?'

Where had the considerate and charming man she'd left that dinner party with gone? Was this the real Dante, or was he just shocked at the news she'd brought?

The idea of being pregnant after a one-night stand

with a man she'd known she'd never see again had been a complete shock to her. So much so that she'd bought all four pregnancy tests in stock at the small pharmacy near her flat in an attempt to convince herself that she'd got it wrong, that their one night of non-committal but passionate sex hadn't resulted in pregnancy. Each time she'd used a test she'd become more panic-stricken.

'Do *you* have any idea how ridiculous it was for you to come here, tell me such news and expect me to stand aside while you leave?' Anger laced his accented words. 'You might have left me once, but it will not happen again, *mia cara.*'

'But *marriage*?' she protested, desperate to make him see how impossible such an idea was. All she'd wanted was for him to know, to be told to his face that he was going to be a father. It would have been what her father would have wanted her to do. 'We don't know anything about each other.'

'I know where you like to be kissed and how very sexy you look when you are naked. I think that is a good enough start, no?'

He smiled a slow, seductive smile and her heart almost stopped beating as she remembered how he had kissed her, how she'd all but begged for more, not wanting him to stop, wanting only to lose herself in the oblivion of the passion he'd showed her.

'Exactly the kind of answer I'd expect from a man like you.' Her temper fired and she drew in a deep breath, challenging the charm he seemed so incredibly capable of even in such a situation.

His eyes darkened and his brows furrowed together. 'A man like me?' His accented words were filled with suspicion.

'There must be *some* truth in that article in *Celebrity*

Spy!' She faltered as his eyes narrowed and she knew she'd touched a raw nerve. But hadn't he charmed her, seduced her, all without them even exchanging names?

'Do you normally believe everything inside such magazines?'

He moved fractionally closer and she resisted the urge to step back, to keep him from invading her space with the power of his masculinity.

'No, of course not.' She snapped the words out quickly, and judging from the smile which lingered on his lips he knew he too had hit the target.

'I would also suggest you change your reading material to something more…how shall I say it?…salubrious.'

Thankfully he stepped away, and she let out a breath she had no idea she'd been holding, but the urge to justify herself was too great. 'I don't normally read it. I was flicking through it whilst waiting at an employment agency.'

'Employment agency?' He turned his attention back to her instantly, those incredibly sexy eyes full of mistrust.

She bit down hard, inwardly cursing her wayward tongue. The last thing she wanted him to know was that she was no longer employed because of their night together, but she'd walked into a trap of her own making.

'I no longer have a permanent contract. The dinner party in London was a one-off.'

'So,' he said, and there was a hint of triumph in that one word. 'You are without a job and pregnant?'

She looked at him warily and corrected him quickly. 'Between jobs.'

'And will you easily find another job as your pregnancy progresses? I think not, *cara.'*

The undeniable self-assurance in his voice irritated

her more than she cared to admit—because he was right. Hadn't that been her worry as she'd tossed and turned every night since discovering she was pregnant? Maybe if she was still living in Sydney, where she'd grown up, she'd be able to find a job. But she wasn't in Sydney. She'd come to her mother's city of birth, London, and she knew nobody. And, as much as she wanted to return to Australia, she needed to stay with her mother.

'That is for me to worry about.' And worrying was just what she would still be doing when she left here. She'd had such a strong bond with her dad that she couldn't imagine bringing a baby into the world and it not knowing its father. It was her experience of a father-daughter relationship which had convinced her that see-ing Dante was the right thing.

She hadn't told her mother about the baby yet, afraid to disappoint her, afraid she'd use her father's memory to make her feel guilty. Would he have been disap-pointed? No, she silently answered herself, but he would have wanted her to do the right thing.

The need to clear her conscience, to tell Dante per-sonally, had fuelled hopes that he would at least ac-knowledge the child and hopefully want to be part of its life. But marriage? That was something she hadn't considered. And even if she had that article in *Celeb-rity Spy!* would have smothered that dream completely. Dante Mancini was a charmer—a playboy with a ruth-less disregard for any kind of commitment.

'You will not have to worry about work now you are to be my wife. I will provide you with everything you and my child can possibly want—and more.'

He stood with his back to the amazing view of Rome, with the winter sunshine sliding in around him, making reading his expression difficult. But she had no doubt how fierce the darkness of his eyes was.

'I do not want to marry you.' She injected attitude into each word, desperate to push home her point.

'It's not negotiable, *cara*. I am in need of a wife and you are carrying my child—which makes you the perfect choice.'

He walked towards her, away from the sunshine which had temporarily concealed his expression, and the determination she saw on his handsome face made her heart sink. She had very little energy left to fight with.

'In need of a wife?' She stumbled over the word 'wife', hardly able to believe he wanted *her* to become his wife. How could a self-professed playboy—a man who had the wealth, power and looks to have any woman he wanted—want to marry *her*?

'I am in negotiations for a business deal which I can only pull off if I am seen to be a man with family values. I need a wife—a woman I can be seen publicly with, and one who can be discreet. Because that untimely piece in *Celebrity Spy!* has made those negotiations somewhat difficult. What better way to prove I am a man of family honour than to stand by the woman who is carrying my child?'

'You make it *all* sound like a business deal.'

'That, *cara*, is precisely what it will be. You came for money and support and you will now get both—providing we are seen out in public as the perfect couple. The world must believe we are madly in love. In return you will have the honour of being the woman who tamed Dante Mancini.'

Dante looked at her, saw her face pale and watched her eyes close, provoking images of her beneath him as passion had driven her wild and he'd unwittingly claimed her as his. Now she would pay the price of acting the part of a seductress when she'd been nothing more than an innocent virgin. She'd pay the price with two words. *I do.*

When her eyes opened, seconds later, the spark of annoyance was back within their sea-green depths. With her shy blushes and understated clothes she certainly didn't look or act like the kind of woman he would date, let alone fall for, but she had on that night in London. He might have scoffed at Benjamin Carter's suggestion last night of using the discreet agency run by the American matchmaker Elizabeth Young to find him a suitable wife, but now he would definitely call upon the agency's services. He needed to transform the Australian redhead who carried his child back into the woman he'd met in London.

'Honour? You overrate yourself, *signor.* If it is to be a business deal and not a true marriage I will accept—with one condition.'

'*You* do not make the conditions.' This was not something he was used to. Women dictating to him. It was unheard of. He was always in control, always laying down the rules.

'I will make all the conditions I want.'

Her flippant tone almost pushed him too far, reminding him just how much his head throbbed with alcohol-induced pain.

'It is obvious that your need of a wife is far greater than my need to tell you that you are going to be a father.'

'*Molto bene.* Name your terms.' Angrily he crossed the room and sat behind his desk, leaning his arms on its clutter-free surface and fixing her with a warning glare.

'The *marriage* will be in name only and it will be ended after an agreed time. Once you have duped the world into thinking you are a reformed character and have secured your business deal, I assume.'

She stood in the centre of his office, her long legs snagging his attention, making him think things he had no right to be thinking—especially as he was negotiating a deal with her. A deal that would save his reputation and enrich his business—*and* claim her as his.

'Va bene.' He nodded his agreement. So far she spoke sense. He didn't want to be married and had never contemplated it. All he needed right now was to change the way the gossips thought of him, prove he could be a family man if he chose to be and ultimately finalise the deal that would put his company at the top of the renewable energies industry. He also needed to calm the fears of their charity and fix any other negative impact of that damning article.

'And you will play an active part in the child's life.'

Her words fell into the suddenly large gap which separated them, highlighting how very different they were.

His brows rose. How could he play an active part in the child's life when he'd been solely responsible for his younger brother's untimely death? He wasn't fit to be a brother, let alone a father. He couldn't commit to giving his son or daughter anything other than material things. His emotions had frozen and shut down the day his father had walked out on them. Alessio's death was proof of that.

She must have sensed his reluctance because she stepped closer. 'I want nothing more than that. If you cannot agree then we do not have a deal and I will leave right now.'

He took a deep breath, forcing back the guilt and regret from the past. He had to think of this as just another deal. One like the many he made each year. He couldn't open the wounds of his past. But as he looked at Piper he suspected it was already too late. She was the key that had turned in the door he'd long ago slammed shut.

He'd never longed for a woman once his desire had been quenched, but Piper had changed that and it was a change he wasn't happy about. Reluctantly he admitted he would have to accept her terms. If he didn't marry her and took another wife she'd have an even bigger story to sell and more damage to do. Worse than that, he would be guilty of turning his back on his child, and he'd pay any price not to do that.

'We have a deal. I will have it drawn up into a contract by tomorrow.'

For a moment she looked lost, as if she'd expected a big battle. Little did she know that was just what it was for him—but it was his battle and he would fight it alone. He didn't need anyone—least of all a woman who threatened everything he'd turned his back on after the revelations exposed by Alessio's death.

'Then, as we have concluded our business, I will go to my hotel.' She picked up a bag from beside the chair she'd been sitting in when he arrived. If that was all her luggage she really hadn't intended on staying in Rome long. *Long enough to turn my world on its head.* If she thought she could just walk away now, she'd got it all wrong.

He sprang from the seat. 'You are not going anywhere except to my apartment—with me.'

'That is totally unnecessary,' she said, and pulled the somewhat battered bag, which bore no resemblance to the designer bags his women usually had, onto her shoulder. She moved towards the door and once again he found himself needing to stop this woman from leaving.

'We are lovers, are we not?' He lowered his voice, smiling to see the blush which crept over her face at the way he spoke. 'And if we are to be believed as such you will not stay in a budget hotel.'

'How do you know it's a budget hotel?'

Indignation flared to life in her voice and her eyes and he knew he'd scored a point in this particular battle.

'I merely assumed.' He shrugged and looked at her, liking the way her lips pressed together tightly as she fought to hold back her retort. A fight she soon lost.

'Well, don't,' she snapped at him, then lowered her gaze briefly before meeting his once more.

'This is a business deal—one which will legitimise my child. A child that will be the heir to all I own. You will have every luxury, Piper, and my word that nothing else will happen between us.'

Piper gulped back the disappointment. *Nothing else would happen between them.* She should be pleased. It was exactly what she'd asked for, what she'd wanted, but a part of her ached with the pain of it. She wasn't his type. The article in *Celebrity Spy!* had left her in no doubt of that. But the passion which had ravaged them that night in London must have meant something.

'That is all I want,' she lied, desperate that he wouldn't detect even a hint of her dismay. She had to remain strong and firm. He couldn't know she'd often thought of those few hours which had changed her life even before she'd known she was pregnant.

'*Va bene.* It is settled. I will escort you to my apartment now—you look tired and in need of rest.'

As he looked at her she could almost believe he was

genuinely concerned, but to fall for such an idea would be her undoing and she had to remain strong.

'I think it would be better if I booked into a hotel.' Her words faded to a whisper at the black look on his handsome face, which appeared more severe due to the shadow of stubble he was sporting.

'How can we be seen as lovers, about to become engaged, if you are not living in my apartment and, as far as the world is concerned, sleeping in my bed?' He shrugged in that nonchalant way which had attracted her the first night she'd seen him. 'It would not be very convincing, *mia cara*.'

Piper pushed her fingers through her hair, trying to control the emotions which were running riot inside her. Emotions she knew full well were intensified by her pregnancy. Why did she feel so let down, so disillusioned? He'd offered to stand by her, support her financially, and most importantly to be a part of their child's life even if he wasn't a part of hers. So why was she fighting the urge to cry? She had what she'd come for—and more.

She dragged in a sharp breath and looked up at him as he approached from her left side—her blind side—startling her when he touched her gently on her arm, as he had done several times already.

'I didn't mean to startle you,' he said softly.

Too softly. Her urge to give in to tiredness and tears intensified.

'Come. You need to rest. You must have left London at an early hour this morning.'

She allowed herself to be guided to the office door, and with his arm lingering around her waist he walked to his secretary's desk, issuing a flurry of Italian instructions which were met with curious gazes directed at her from the shocked older woman, unsettling her further. Was she so far below the kind of woman he usually dated that even his secretary was shocked?

Everything seemed to take on a glow of unreality as he escorted her out of the offices and to a waiting car. Moments later they were ensconced in the car, moving quickly through the streets of Rome as car horns sounded insistently around them. She wanted to see the sights, but the ride in the car was making her feel unsteady, and all she could do was sit back in the soft leather seats.

On her right, she felt Dante watching her. She could feel the scrutiny of his gaze and almost hear his unspoken questions. Everything about being with Dante again was unlocking all those emotions she'd hidden away as she'd left that hotel in the early hours.

As she got out of the car the tall buildings of the old town towered over her and blocked out the winter sun. She looked up at an impressive building which must have seen many things through history, unable to believe what she'd agreed to.

He took her bag from her. 'This way. My apartment is on the top floor and offers stunning views of the city from the roof terrace. Have you been in Rome before?'

The light and easy way he spoke was in complete contrast to the way her heart was thumping. What had she done to herself? What had she agreed to? Marriage, be it in name only or not, to a man she barely knew?

'No. Europe always seemed too far from Australia to think of.'

It had been a trip her mother had wanted to do. She'd tried to convince her father, but he'd never wanted to leave Australia, saying he didn't need to go so far when he had all he needed at home. As he'd said those words he'd looked at her, and now Piper questioned if her mother's need to return to England had been the start of their marriage problems.

Dante held the front door open for her and she walked into the cool shade of the old building, trying to leave the memories and questions she'd never have answered outside.

'Yet you were in London when we met?'

'I'd only been there for a year. My mother wanted to return to her native country after...' She floundered for a moment, thinking of the day her father had suddenly died. Exactly one year to the day when she'd met Dante. 'My father was Australian, my mother British, and after he died she wanted to be with her elderly mother so we left Sydney. Sadly, Grandma passed away a few months ago.'

Dante scrutinised her as he waited for the elevator and she wondered if her true feelings were showing clearly on her face, despite the calm and matter-of-fact way she'd imparted the story of her beloved father's death.

'And you were brought up in Sydney?'

She was glad when the elevator doors opened, diverting his attention. She'd never known anything *but* Sydney. It was not only where she'd grown up, but where she'd been happiest. But all that had changed when her father had been killed in a car accident. The senseless accident had happened not even a year after he'd been told he was in remission from cancer. The injustice of it made her gulp back the tears which threatened.

'Can't you tell from the accent?' She laughed off the pain of those memories, wanting to move the conversation away from her. This wasn't about her any more. It was about what was best for the baby. Her father had stood by her mother when she'd fallen pregnant and they'd been happy together. But obviously it hadn't been enough for her mother, because she'd started to make plans to return to London soon after the accident.

'It's a nice accent.' He smiled at her and she wondered if he'd sensed her unease, but his next words obliterated that thought. 'And very sexy too, when you are consumed by desire.'

'You should keep such comments for the women you date.'

The words left her before she could stop them, let alone think about what they meant to her. The thought of him dating other women made her heart heavy, but she had to push that aside. Their marriage was to be nothing more than a business deal.

He walked from the elevator, pulling out a key, and turned to look at her as he stopped outside his apartment door. 'Exclusivity is something I will demand from you if this deal is going to work for us.'

That wouldn't be a problem as far as she was concerned. Her one spontaneous and totally out of character affair had already caused her more trouble than she'd ever bargained on.

'I should impose the same on you, but I doubt a man like you can be exclusive to *any* woman.'

Dante didn't miss the crisp tartness in her voice. The subject was something he'd already given thought to on the drive to his apartment. He would have to be faithful to his new fiancée and, given that his body still heated at the memory of hers, it wouldn't be a challenge. The biggest problem would be to ensure he didn't repeat what had happened in London. She had made it clear this was to be only a business deal.

If he portrayed himself to the world as a caring and faithful man, in love with the woman who was to be his wife, he would not only clinch the deal he'd almost lost but wipe out the reputation that for years he hadn't cared about. If he didn't, the future of The Hope Foundation, the charity he wholeheartedly supported, would hang in the balance.

The three other businessmen who supported the charity were about to do the same. Zayn and Xander had agreed that Benjamin's suggestion that they settle down was the only way. He'd watched on, uncharacteristically drowning his misgivings in a bottle of whisky, as the ghosts of his past had taunted him that he'd never be able to be responsible for another person without hurting them, forcing them to leave him.

Now he was responsible for a woman who should have been his for just a few hours of mind-blowing sex. Not only that, he was responsible for the child she carried—*his* child. Could he put himself through that? Could he engage the emotions he'd switched off and risk losing everything again?

'You will have my full and undivided attention at all times. We are in love, no?' As he looked down at her that spark of lust, a sexual chemistry too strong to deny, arced between them. He saw her eyes darken, watched her lips part, and his body responded in the only way possible to such a blatant invitation.

'Nothing can ever happen between us again, Dante.'

Her whisper cracked with desire, and in normal circumstances he would have laughed softly, pulled her against him and kissed her into submission. But these were not normal circumstances. This wasn't just a meaningless affair that would end as soon as the sun rose the next morning.

'I have agreed to our terms.' He unlocked his door and stood back for her to enter, smiling down at her in an attempt to hide the conflicting emotions warring within him. 'A marriage in name only that will give us both what we want.'

'More than that, Dante.'

She stood outside, as if crossing the threshold to his home was the last thing she wanted to do. To have her permanently in his life was not what he wanted, but he had his reasons for making this deal. Just as she had hers.

'It will give our child what it deserves.'

The mention of the baby shocked any response from him and he turned and walked into his apartment—a place he'd never taken a woman before, preferring the anonymity of hotel rooms which he could leave when he was ready.

'Tomorrow you will sign a contact.' His irritation at the situation he found himself in sounded in his words—even he could hear that.

Not only was he inviting a woman into his home and his life—permanently—he was giving himself the biggest challenge of all. One he wasn't sure he could master. He would have to invest himself, his emotions, in a child. How could he do that when the pain of Alessio's loss, the guilt of his inability to be what someone else needed, still festered in his dormant heart?

'Until then you will have to trust me when I say that I will be the perfect gentleman, and that you may sleep soundly in my bed.'

'In your bed?' The few hesitant steps she'd taken into his domain faltered to a stop.

'Alone,' he added.

She really was adamant that they would not be repeating those hot, sultry hours in London. So be it. He didn't want the added complication of lust becoming more than that.

'We've settled this. As my lover you need to be seen here, at all times of the day and night. What the outside world will never know is that I will sleep there.'

He gestured to the second bedroom, which served as his office. Last night, if one of the other three men had suggested he'd be taking a woman into his life and sleeping in his spare room in order to salvage his reputation and that of his supported charity, he would have laughed.

'I'm not sure… I'll find a hotel.'

'That is not an option any longer, *mia cara*. You should not have come all this way, imparted such news and then expected me not to put my terms on any arrangement made.'

The late night and early start were finally catching up with him, and all he wanted was to shut the door on the world and relax. But first he had to contact Elizabeth Young and ascertain if her agency offered the services he required. He needed to transform the plain and ordinary woman before him into a fiancée that would bring the gossips to a tongue-tied halt.

'I can't take your bed.'

'*Va bene*, then I will share it with you if it makes you feel better.' He stifled a smile at her shock.

'No,' she said, and she all but flounced past him into the apartment, her attitude hinting that the woman he'd met in London was still lingering inside her, waiting to be drawn out. If he dared to find her.

'Then at last we understand one another. I suggest you make yourself at home. I have work to continue with.'

Never had he ever thought he would be inviting a woman into his home, into his life, and telling her to make herself comfortable. The idea was unnerving, but reluctantly he knew it was necessary.

It would make him part of his child's life. It was a child he'd never wanted, but despite that he already knew he would do anything for it.

CHAPTER THREE

PIPER WOKE THE next morning, the soft sheets caressing her skin as she stretched, and then realisation hit. This wasn't her bed. She sat upright quickly and looked around the room, momentarily not recalling actually getting into bed. In fact she couldn't remember much after arriving yesterday with Dante.

She'd been so tired. The confrontation with Dante had sapped any remaining strength she'd had—which had been very little after weeks of barely sleeping because of the situation she'd found herself plunged into. But right now her biggest worry was the fact that she was in bed, wearing only her underwear, and had no recollection of getting there.

As if her thoughts had summoned him Dante knocked lightly on the bedroom door. *'Buongiorno.'*

His deep and undeniably sexy voice came through the door and the image of him that it conjured in her mind was immediate and vivid—but she had to remember the man she'd confronted yesterday was the same as the one described in *Celebrity Spy!* He'd also been suffering the effects of alcohol, probably from partying the previous night with glamorous women. It had shocked her that he was so far from the loving man she'd met briefly in London.

'Come in,' she said, far more boldly than she felt, and tugged the sheet tighter against her. Had she undressed in a tired trance or had he removed her clothes?

The door clicked open and Dante entered. The hint of stubble which had coloured his face yesterday was gone. The clean-shaven look reminded her of the man she'd lost more than just her virginity to.

'I trust you slept well, *cara*?'

'I did—thank you.' She wasn't going to give him the satisfaction of asking if he was the one who had undressed her and pulled the luxurious sheets over her instead of leaving her lying on the bed. Her only memory from last night was of lying there for just a few minutes.

'Good. We have a busy day ahead of us.'

He walked closer, his expression bland and unyielding, and try as she might she couldn't help but admire the way his shirt was all but moulded to his body. A body she remembered clearly and a body she wanted to know again. Except that would be too dangerous— now that she knew who he really was and what he was capable of.

'We do?' She hoped the flush that crept over her cheeks wouldn't give her away.

'*Sì*. I have the necessary paperwork for our deal, awaiting your signature, then we can go shopping.'

A hint of mischief sparked in his eyes as he turned his full attention to her as if he knew she was being a tease but refused to rise to it.

'Shopping?' she asked casually as she sat back against the soft pillows. If only she didn't feel as if she'd walked into the pride leader's den. 'Why do we need to go shopping?'

'For the single most important item, if this deal is to achieve its aim. A ring.'

He moved towards the bed and she had to work hard to resist the temptation to pull the sheets tighter still against her—whether to hide her state of undress or protect her heart as it fluttered at his increasingly dominating presence, she couldn't tell. Either way, she wouldn't do it—wouldn't give him the satisfaction of knowing just how much he could unbalance her with one look.

'Of course.' Her nonchalant tone was a total contrast to the racing of her heart and the flutter of the butterflies which had taken residence in her tummy. 'I will join you shortly.'

'Breakfast is waiting for you.' His dark eyes fixed her intently to the spot and instantly she was back on that bed in the hotel room in London as he'd stood and looked at her, desire and passion so tangible in the air that she hadn't wanted the moment ever to end.

'Thank you.' She dragged her mind back from that night. She would have to put such notions well and truly to one side if she was going to survive this deal she'd struck. Dante didn't have feelings for her. She was merely a means to an end. A way to seal his deal. He was exactly the inscrutable businessman *Celebrity Spy!* had portrayed him as being.

The trouble was she also knew he was a skilled lover—which was what had earned him such a scandalous reputation with women—and a rebellious part of her yearned to experience that man again. After all, her current situation couldn't get much worse. She was pregnant, jobless, and being forced into marriage as part of a business deal. It was ludicrous when all she'd wanted to do was make him aware of his child and ease her conscience.

She watched as he turned and left, unable to pull her gaze away from the broad shoulders covered in a pale blue shirt that somehow emphasised every last muscle her fingers annoyingly remembered tracing on his back.

Once the door had clicked closed she slid out of bed. Although her tummy protested its emptiness she headed for the shower, determined that when they went out later she would look at least a little bit more glamorous and like the women he'd been pictured with throughout that article as proof of his Casanova lifestyle.

The problem was she didn't really know how to achieve such glamour—that was why she'd been sent out to the hairdresser's and lent a dress that day she'd been told she would have to stand in for a colleague for one night and be hostess for a dinner party in London. Whilst she'd enjoyed feeling so different, it hadn't really been *her*. It was a different Piper who had gained the interest of Dante Mancini, one of the world's most debauched bachelors, but it was the real Piper who'd fallen for him right there and then.

Dante stood on his terrace, looking out over Rome as the city became its bustling usual self. Sounds of the street drifted up while he sipped his coffee and waited for Piper. On the table inside, which he'd instructed to be laid for two, was the contract. Once that was signed there would be no going back. He would be responsible not only for Piper, a woman who intrigued him more than any other, but for a child. A responsibility he wasn't sure he could meet when the demons of Alessio's death still plagued him.

'I'm sorry I kept you.'

Piper's sexy voice, with its delicious accent, dragged him from his dark thoughts.

'I took the liberty of arranging an assortment of choices for breakfast,' he said.

'That sounds wonderful.'

She smiled up at him and he instantly remembered the moment he'd first seen that smile directed at him. He'd walked into the party, not really wanting to be there, and he'd seen her. Despite the fact that she'd been working she'd looked glamorous and very sexy in a black silk dress which had caressed her curvy figure, making him want to touch her, hold her.

He'd wanted her from that moment and had used his charm to achieve just that. Little had he known that his usual sense of control and self-preservation would fail him the moment they first kissed.

'Is it not usual for women to feel ill in the mornings when they are pregnant?' He couldn't keep the scepticism from his voice as the thoughts which had invaded his dreams last night clouded round him once more. He had no proof that she was pregnant. He'd taken her word not only for that, but for the fact that *he* was the father. He would take the advice his legal team had given him when drawing up the contract and have his own doctor confirm the pregnancy.

'Yes.' She smiled at him again, apparently oblivious to his suspicions. 'Thankfully I don't seem too troubled by that and I hope it stays that way.'

'*Bene*. First we eat—then we will deal with the contract.' He pulled out a chair for her and waited for her to sit, but knew instantly that had been a mistake as the scent of her freshly washed hair mingled with her perfume, invading his senses so fast he wanted to lower his head, kiss her hair and inhale her, then scoop her up and take her to his bed.

He'd forced himself to walk away from her last night, but could he do it again?

He stepped back. Away from such temptation. Nothing could happen between them. This wasn't a fling. Nothing about this was casual at all, and the last thing he needed was to complicate it further and get involved. He could never be involved.

He watched her as she ate, realising he hadn't ever had breakfast with a woman he hadn't slept with the previous night. In fact he rarely even had breakfast with women, preferring instead to leave the bed and give a very clear message. So why did sitting across the table from a woman who'd been so tired he'd had to help her to undress before tucking her into his bed and then gallantly leaving her alone feel so inviting?

'I'm sorry about last night,' she said, her shyness returning as she blushed. 'Falling asleep like that, I mean. You must think I'm very rude.'

'I think you were tired from travelling in your condition.' He poured fresh coffee and tried hard not to allow the image of her asleep on his bed, hair splayed out around her, to return to his mind and torment him. She'd looked so vulnerable, so beautiful, and all he'd wanted to do was look after her. But could he do that? He hadn't been able to look after his own brother, so how could a woman he'd just met be any different?

'Well, I'm refreshed and feeling much more myself today, thank you.'

'Prego.' He pushed the black thoughts away and picked up the contract which he'd seen her glance at several times, as if it was a dog that might bite her at any moment. 'This has been drawn up according to the terms we discussed yesterday, and once signed it will bind us together in our deal for a minimum of two years.'

'And the baby?'

Her question rocked him but he kept his focus, portraying outward control even if inside he was far from controlled.

'I will be a part of my child's life for ever.'

The firmness and passion in his voice shocked him—as did the realisation that it was what he wanted. His child wouldn't be born illegitimate, with the odds stacked against him. His child would have everything he could possibly give it to succeed in life.

'But we will both be free to end the marriage in two years and during that time we can live separately—once the main objectives of the deal are achieved, that is.'

'The main objective for you being to secure a business deal?'

The accusation in her voice hit its mark, making his requirement seem insignificant in the face of hers. The deal *had* been his initial motivation, but as the implications of their few steamy hours together that night had sunk in he'd known he would do anything for his child. There was no way he would walk out and never look back. He was not his father.

'*Di preciso.*' Briefly English failed him as the truth of his thoughts penetrated deep into him. 'Exactly. But if I do not secure my business deals then I will not have the means to give my child much.'

'You could give it love.'

Her words smarted in the wound she was opening. One he'd long since thought healed.

Love was the one thing he *couldn't* give. Anyone he'd given that to had gone from his life. His father, his brother... With the exception of his feelings for his mother, love was one emotion he could not do, because by doing so he'd risk everything. Love hadn't stopped his father walking away when he and Alessio were young. It hadn't stopped his brother from falling in with those gangs, and it hadn't helped at all when for years he'd not even known where Alessio was. It certainly hadn't helped when he'd discovered the truth of his brother's death.

Love was a futile and wasted emotion.

'My child, my heir, will have everything it needs— of that you can be assured.'

She looked at him, those green eyes smouldering with doubt—a doubt which beat wildly within him right now. Did she have any idea what she was asking of him with those words?

'That is all I want for my child, Dante. The love and security of knowing its father, of being able to have a good relationship with him as I did with mine.'

Piper tried to push thoughts of her father aside. Now, in the face of Dante's scepticism, was not the time to remember just how much she missed her father. The grief of losing him was still raw after all these months. It was why she'd sought solace in Dante's arms that night, why she'd given herself to him—that and the powerful attraction which had sparked between them.

'This is the contract.'

He pushed the papers across the table to her, his hand lingering on it as if he wasn't sure he actually wanted her to have it. She saw the gold of his signet ring gleam in the lights above.

She sighed, not sure she should be signing anything, but she couldn't stay like this, in limbo from reality, not knowing what was going to happen. At least this way her child stood some chance of having a father who was around. He passed her a pen and she looked again at his ring. It was engraved with the letter A. Was that the initial of a past lover?

'One signature on each copy,' he said firmly, pulling her back from her thoughts.

'There,' she said as her name sprawled across the line. 'It's official.'

'*Bene.* Now we will need to purchase a ring.'

His words brought her crashing back to the present.

'Is that necessary when it is only an engagement for show and a marriage on paper?'

'*Sì, cara,* it is. As are a few other changes.'

'Changes?' Trepidation filled her. What else did he have planned?

He walked towards her, his eyes seeming to devour her, sending sparks of awareness all over her body, just as they'd done that night in London.

'You have changed, *cara,* since we met in London.'

She frowned, taking in his words. Was she not good enough for him? The spiteful rejection from her days at school rushed back at her. Then, her lack of vision in one eye had been all too obvious, and some of her classmates had thought it amusing to taunt her. Now, after the operations her father had insisted she have, her disability was not so obvious. Although the ability to see with her left eye would never be possible, it was far less noticeable.

'This is who I am, Dante, not the woman you met in London.'

'I disagree. But right now I need to buy you a ring—one that will announce to the world that you are my intended bride.'

'And make you look like a man with *true family values*?' She couldn't keep the barb out of her voice.

'*Di preciso.* Now, if you are ready, we shall go and make our purchase.'

* * *

Half an hour later Dante's car arrived in the centre of Rome, in an area which thronged with locals and tourists alike. The winter sun was warm and for a moment she relished it after having spent the last few months experiencing her first British winter.

'This way,' he said as he leant close to her ear, and his words sent a whisper of tingles down her spine as he spoke.

At least this time he was standing on her right side and she'd known he was there—although that wasn't entirely a good thing if the way she'd reacted to his nearness was anything to go by.

'I have arranged a private consultation with one of Rome's most renowned jewellers.'

To her surprise he took her hand as they began walking through the crowded streets. When had he arranged that? With a sinking heart she realised that the father of her child, the man she'd agreed to marry, moved in a very different world from the one she was used to. He could just make a call and demand what he wanted.

Nerves skittered inside her tummy like erratic butterflies as he stopped outside a shop whose windows were a source of curiosity for quite a number of people, and she blushed as some glanced their way when Dante pushed open the door. Instantly they were greeted by a member of staff, but the fast-flowing Italian became too difficult for her very limited knowledge of the language.

'We are honoured to be of service to you, *signorina.*'

The man's English proved to be better than her Italian and made her feel a little less apprehensive. At least she would know what was being said.

'If you'd like to come this way, Signor Mancini?'

Dante stood back and waited for her to follow the

older gentleman, and within minutes they were in a small but elegantly furnished room.

'I have followed your instructions, *signor*, on what the *signorina* prefers, and have arranged a selection of rings for you to view.'

Piper tried hard to keep the smile on her lips, to appear as if this was real instead of the nightmare it had suddenly become. She had to remember this wasn't an engagement in the true sense of the word. Just as the contract she had signed that morning reminded her that their marriage would not be a real one. Putting a ring on her finger was no different from putting her signature on the contract he'd so insistently laid out on the breakfast table.

'Piper?'

Dante's voice, close to her left side, startled her again. 'I'm sorry,' she said, trying to quell the racing of her heart—which she suspected had more to do with the man himself than with being startled. Quickly recovering, she gestured to the table and the array of rings set on a deep blue velvet display tray. 'I've never seen anything quite like this.'

'This is just the beginning,' he said softly.

The darkness of his eyes shone with unwavering adoration and for a moment she was almost fooled—almost believed that he did love her and wanted nothing other than to make her his.

The harsh reality was quite different. It was not for any kind of sentimental reason and certainly not out of love.

'This is enough for now.' She blushed beneath his practised charm and when his brows flicked suggestively her stomach tied itself in knots and her breath caught audibly in her throat.

'We should choose the ring now, *cara*, before I forget why we are here and kiss you.'

He looked at her, the intense blackness in his eyes smothering the caramel-brown she found so attractive. She could smell his aftershave and found her lips parting of their own free will as her breathing quickened and her pulse raced. Shyly she looked up at him as he moved closer still. Panic skittered through her. He was going to kiss her—here, in public.

A polite cough from the older man thankfully diverted Dante's attention from her and for a moment she couldn't get enough breath into her lungs. She focused on regaining her composure and took a seat at the desk, giving the glittering array of rings her undivided attention. She looked from one large stone to another, hardly able to believe she was sitting there, within touching distance of so many valuable and beautiful gems.

She felt Dante move behind her and her whole body heated from his nearness. But when he placed his hand on her shoulder and leant over her she thought she might pass out. Why was she behaving like this? He didn't want her for anything other than to make him look good in a business deal. She would stake everything on the fact that he didn't want to be a father. His reaction to her news had been cold and detached. Marriage had been the last thing she'd expected to hear him demand as she'd sat in his office yesterday, waiting for him to arrive, having been assured by his secretary that he wasn't usually late.

'Select whichever one you want.' His voice was close to her left ear, but from the heat of his body against her back and the scorching of his hand on her shoulder she knew he was there. How could she not when her whole body had come to life?

'They are all beautiful.'

She turned her head to try and look at him, and in doing so found his face very close to hers. So close that he could kiss her, press his lips to hers, with only the slightest effort. His gaze locked onto hers and she couldn't look away. Not even when he lowered his head and very gently brushed his lips over hers.

Her eyes closed and her lips softened beneath his before he pulled back slightly and with endearing tenderness brushed his fingers over her cheek. 'You outshine them all.'

Don't be fooled. The voice of reason fought to be heard inside her head as that kiss, that gentle and brief feel of his lips on hers, unlocked everything she'd been trying to deny since that night in London.

Piper turned away and tried hard to focus on the rings before her as their gleam blurred and tears threatened. Now was *not* a time to give in to emotions.

She reached out and picked up a ring. 'I like this one.'

Dante took the ring from her, then moved to her side, took her left hand and slipped the ring onto her finger. It glinted as it sat, a perfect fit, on her third finger. She was so stunned by the sight of it she couldn't speak, couldn't say anything, and she certainly couldn't look up at Dante—not when tears threatened to spill down her cheeks like a waterfall.

'I think my bride has made her choice.' His voice was deep and accented and so sexy—just as it had been that night in London. It had haunted her since he'd whispered such beautiful words in her ears as they'd made love that first and only night.

Piper couldn't function, and she sat in a state of bewilderment as the older man fussed around them and then packed up the ring in the most elaborate box. All she could do was watch as Dante produced his credit card and paid for the ring, which effectively meant he'd paid for *her*, a bargaining tool for the deal he just had to win.

But to her the price was much higher. To her this was all about her child—the only reason she'd accepted such a deal.

CHAPTER FOUR

IT HAD BEEN three days since Dante had bought the ring, which had sealed the deal far more conclusively than any contract she'd signed. Each night she'd slept alone in his bed, and not once since that light but lingering kiss in the jeweller's had he tried to get close to her again. Neither had he done anything to suggest he wanted their arrangement to be more than a marriage on paper. He'd made it clear that whatever had exploded into life so spectacularly between them in London was over as far as he was concerned.

That kiss as they'd chosen the ring and those gestures had all been for the benefit of the jeweller. Her shock at the disappointment that knowledge had brought still weighed heavily on her as she stood in the apartment while Dante finished a call.

She felt as uneasy and out of place as she had that first morning as she listened to him, and then registered that he was talking in English.

'Xander will also call you,' he said, and glanced up, seeing her for the first time. He ended the call and turned his full attention to her. *'Buongiorno, cara.'*

The sensual depth in his voice did little to assuage her disillusioned mind-set.

'Buongiorno,' she replied, testing his language and

liking the feel of it almost as much as the approval which showed clearly in his sexy dark eyes.

Don't go there, Piper, she silently warned herself, determined to remember why she'd flown to Rome in search of a man whose name she hadn't known until she'd seen that article.

'I trust you slept well.' As usual he was the epitome of charm and courtesy.

'I did, thank you,' she replied, and her guilt at keeping him from his bed made looking at him as they sat at the table almost impossible.

'Bene.'

He poured her coffee, but for the first time since she'd discovered she was pregnant the aroma made her feel queasy and she opted for a glass of water instead. She looked up at him as he spoke again.

'You have a busy day ahead of you.'

She tried to work out what it was she should be doing. For three days she'd been cooped up here in his apartment, more like a prisoner than a guest. She'd called her mother, who had wanted her to go straight home, as had Katie and Jo, her friends in Australia, when they'd emailed. But where *was* home? In London with her mother? In Sydney with her happy past? Or here in Rome with the father of her child?

Confusion added to the feeling of nausea. 'I do?'

'Sì. I have arranged for someone to help you select a new wardrobe of clothes.'

She watched as he drank his coffee, oblivious to anything else except what *he* wanted. He certainly hadn't noticed she couldn't face any food this morning.

'I don't need new clothes.' She forced the words out, trying to focus her mind and not show this man any weakness—something she'd learnt long ago shouldn't be done.

'You are now my fiancée, Piper, and whilst you looked every bit the kind of woman who would ensnare my interest when we met in London, you would not convince many people now. For you to fit in with my world there need to be some changes.'

'Well, I'm sorry to disappoint.' She couldn't keep the spike of hurt from her voice, especially after she had already been making an effort. 'I don't happen to have a wardrobe of party clothes with me. It's not what I had in mind when I came to Rome.'

'No, I am aware of that—which is why I have arranged for some help.' The firm tone of his voice brooked no argument.

'Oh.' The croissant she'd just taken one small piece from in the hope of settling her stomach became like dust in her mouth. So she wasn't good enough for him as she was? Retaliation surfaced. 'I hardly see the point when I'm not going to fit into things in a few months.'

'The *point*—' he fixed her with those intent eyes '—is that our engagement be believed genuine, and presently I do not think it will be. I have arranged for Elizabeth Young, a professional matchmaker from America, to come to Rome and assist you. Every woman loves shopping, and with my name and funds at your disposal I'm sure you will too.'

So she was to be groomed into shape—moulded into the kind of woman who would fit the role of fiancée for the notorious Dante Mancini? And wouldn't that be for the best, no matter how *used* it made her feel? If she played the role so convincingly that his business acquaintances believed that she and Dante were in love, that she was the woman who'd made him want to settle down and be a father, she would have done her part in their deal. It would leave him no option but to do his and be there for their child—long after their marriage had ended. As stipulated in the contract she'd signed, he would then pay his price.

'Very well.' Her voice was starchy and she saw a smile spread over his lips as she looked across the table at him, trying to remind herself why she'd agreed to this charade. Dante could never be the father figure her own father had been, but could she trust him to take even the smallest amount of interest in his child? If he didn't there was no point in her being here now. 'And when will we be putting this glamorous fiancée to the test?'

His dark eyes sparked dangerously at her last words. 'This evening. We shall attend a party here in Rome. And at the weekend we have been invited to Tuscany by Bettino D'Antonio, which will be the biggest test of our *engagement*. He is the man I intend to seal the business deal with, and this weekend will be the time to reassure him I am a reformed man with family values. He must know you are expecting my child, and that we are in love and engaged to be married.'

She raised a brow haughtily at him, the feeling of being controlled and manipulated uncomfortable. 'So my duties are very clearly defined? I am to look the part of one of the many women you've been pictured with this year alone, while at the same time convincing everyone that what is between us is enough for you to give up your scandalous playboy reputation and settle down?'

The angry glitter in his eyes left her in no doubt that she'd hit the intended mark and was now in control—of this evening's outing at least.

'Elizabeth is the matchmaker Benjamin Carter used.

She is currently in Rome and will meet with you this morning.'

'Benjamin Carter?' Wasn't he also one of the bachelors named and shamed? She tried to recall the others.

'*Sì*, he was featured in that article, along with Zayn Al-Ghamdi and Xander Trakas.'

'And are those men also marrying to save their reputations?'

Suspicion filled her. They couldn't *all* be chasing a big deal, so what was it all about? If her memory served her right, one of them was the ruler of a desert kingdom.

Exasperated with herself for not paying more attention to the piece simply because she'd stumbled upon the identity of the man whose baby she carried, she rebelled against Dante. 'What if I don't want to be turned into one of your women? What if I don't want to change?'

'It is not negotiable, Piper. Elizabeth has my list of instructions on exactly what I want.'

'What *you* want? What about what *I* want?' Already she had lost the small triumph of being in control. How had she ever thought a woman like her could be in control of a man like Dante Mancini? He was ruthless. Just the fact that he was prepared to marry in order to secure a business deal should have set alarm bells ringing. Worry crowded in on her. If Dante was so ruthless, what did this far-fetched situation make *her*?

The answer came instantly. *A mother trying to do the right thing by her child.*

'You gave up that privilege when you signed the contract, *cara*. Right now this is all about salvaging my reputation so that I can seal a deal I've wanted to make for several years.'

'This is not what I intended at all. I should be back in London now, having informed you that you are to be a father—something I felt should be done face to face. I had not for one moment thought you would put forward such a preposterous deal and flaunt me like a trinket, luring someone into a business deal with exactly the kind of man he doesn't want to do business with.'

'Next time you read an article about me in a gossip magazine perhaps you will believe it when I am depicted as a mercenary businessman who lives hard and plays even harder.'

He moved closer to her, his eyes hardening and she knew if she was sensible she'd heed the warning in them.

'I have no scruples, Piper. I will always do whatever is necessary without a thought for anyone who stands in my way.'

'This isn't about *you*,' she gasped, feeling her emotions boiling over in a way she now recognised as part of her pregnancy. 'Or about your barbaric deal. This is about our baby. Your *child*.'

'A child I had no intention of creating.' His denial flew back at her, and the accusation in his voice was clear. 'But right now you are due to meet Elizabeth. This discussion will have to wait.'

He pulled his phone from his pocket and dialled, almost instantly giving instructions in Italian while he picked up papers and put them into his briefcase. He ended the call as he turned back to her, putting on the sunglasses she was beginning to understand were far more than just protection against the sun. They shielded him from everyone, hiding his cold, emotionless eyes.

'My car is waiting.'

The silence in the car as they negotiated the busy streets of Rome was intense to the point of being explosive. The brief conversation that had leapt unwittingly to life between them this morning had exposed all that was wrong with the deal she'd made with this man. They might have shared the most wonderful night of sex, and she might have given him her virginity in a spontaneous act of rebellion against the hand life had dealt her, but she had also fallen just a little bit too hard for him—and she would have to get over that quickly. Having any kind of feelings for a man such as Dante went against all her hopes and dreams for the future. The happy-ever-after ending her father had always promised her was out there, waiting…

Dante was incredibly attractive even now, and his brooding presence dominated the interior of the car as they sat together in the back, where she was powerless to resist the temptation to glance at his handsome profile. How was it possible that *she*, an ordinary girl who'd led a sheltered, protected and happy life in Sydney until her father's death, could fall under the spell of this undisputed pleasure-seeking billionaire bachelor?

Dante could still feel Piper's scrutiny as the car pulled up at outside a boutique he knew first-hand was visited by women from afar. Elizabeth had suggested it when she'd contacted him by email after Benjamin Carter had put the wheels in motion.

Dante hadn't been able to hide his pleasure at Benjamin's shock when he'd called to tell him about Piper and how very convenient it had been that she'd chosen that very day—the day he'd accepted that he needed a wife—to wait in his office, saving him the trouble of selecting a woman. But not only did Piper possess information about him that could destroy him professionally, she was carrying his child. He hadn't told Benjamin he would do anything to protect that child—even give up his bachelor lifestyle.

He got out and went round to Piper's side, aware that opportunistic photographers might be at such locations but hoping against it—at least until his fiancée had assumed again the identity she'd very skilfully used in London. Once she was that hot redhead again, and wearing his ring, he intended to give the press every opportunity to photograph them and spread the good news.

He took her hand, and the hesitation in her step was obvious as they walked into the shop, which he'd instructed would have to be closed to any other shoppers for the duration of their visit.

'Buongiorno, signor...signorina.' If the assistant was surprised at his presence in the shop she hid it very well. 'Signora Young is in my office. Please, this way.'

The assistant's use of English proved that his every request was being followed to the smallest detail. He looked down at Piper, at the glorious red hair which had been piled luxuriously on her head in London but which now fell loose around her shoulders, and felt a moment's hesitation at trying to change her. She was different from his usual choice of woman, enticingly different, and hadn't he become bored with the women of his circle?

He pushed that thought aside as quickly as it had formed. Didn't every woman like to be dressed up, styled by experts and then whisked away to a beauty salon to be pampered? She had a role to play in this deal and he intended she would play it properly.

'I will leave you in the capable hands of Elizabeth.'

He saw her swallow, the movement of her throat giving away the nerves she was trying to hide. It made her look vulnerable and tugged at his conscience—until he remembered the role of confident woman she'd played in London. She had looked confident and comfortable then.

'And what are your instructions for this transformation of your fiancée?'

The spark of fury in her voice only served to bring a smile to his lips, and from the flash of defiance in her eyes it was not a smile she wanted to see.

'Elizabeth has instructions for exactly what is required and she will ensure you know all that is necessary for an evening dinner party. I have seen you poised and elegant, Piper, so I am sure it will be easy for you to act that role once more.'

Before she could formulate any response he knocked on the office door and opened it. The woman who stood and greeted them was dressed simply, in a tan leather jacket over a white blouse and short skirt, and yet had an understated elegance about her. First impressions were important to Dante, and this time he was happy with Benjamin's suggestion to utilise all that Elizabeth Young's company, Leviathan Solutions, could offer.

'Signor Mancini... Ms Riley, good morning.' The woman's smile was warm and friendly as she stepped from behind the desk to greet them.

'*Buongiorno.*'

'I have all your instructions, Signor Mancini, and Piper—may I call you Piper?' She directed the question at Piper, who Dante thought now seemed remarkably relaxed. Was she resigned to the situation she was in? Maybe her insistence that it wasn't needed had been a ploy.

'Yes, of course,' Piper replied, and looked up at him and smiled.

He was shocked to realise it was a genuine smile,

one which lit up her eyes, taking him right back to the moment he'd first seen her at that dinner party in one of London's top hotels. He'd known in that instant that he wanted her—and had set about making it happen, using the champagne and the anonymity of such an evening to achieve just that, with his usual disregard for social proprieties.

'*Bene*, then I shall see you this evening. My car will be at your disposal all day, and will return you to the apartment later this afternoon.'

He had no wish to spend the day judging dresses, shoes and handbags. There were far more important things for him to do, such as finding a way to convince Bettino D'Antonio that making a deal with his business would be beneficial to both of them.

Piper relaxed as the door closed behind Dante and she heard him saying goodbye in the shop. At least nobody else would witness her so-called transformation as his fiancée other than Elizabeth Young, a woman with warm eyes and a friendly smile whom she couldn't help but like instantly, despite her part in all this.

'We should get started,' Elizabeth said, picking up a notepad and pen, and left the office.

Piper, wishing she could achieve that effortless chic style, followed her through the shop into a large changing room adorned with many ornate mirrors.

'Dante's list is extensive. I had already selected several gowns for this evening's dinner party, but the moment I saw you I knew there was one that was perfect.'

Elizabeth's enthusiasm was infectious, and Piper found herself excited as an assistant appeared. She watched in an almost dreamlike state as Elizabeth signalled to a member of the boutique's staff who held up a long bronze dress, adorned with sequins. The assistant held it across her arms as she stood in the dressing room. Piper had never seen such a dress before, let alone worn one. How could Elizabeth think it was perfect for her?

'Bronze will look amazing with your hair, and the dress will accentuate your gorgeous figure.'

Elizabeth's flurry of words held a hint of excitement which transferred itself to Piper. None of this was for real, but it was happening, and she *did* have the role of fiancée to play. Would it be so wrong to get carried away with the fun of all the glamour?

'It's beautiful.' Piper touched the delicate fabric as the assistant held it for her, wondering how it would feel to wear such a dress. Should she tell Elizabeth that her so-called gorgeous figure would be short-lived? 'It's *very* beautiful. But I'm not sure it will be suitable.'

'Just try it,' encouraged Elizabeth as she ushered Piper behind a changing screen.

Piper looked at her reflection in the large gilded mirror moments later, not even sure if the woman who gazed back at her was real. How could one dress make her look and feel so different?

'It's perfect.' Elizabeth's no-nonsense tone halted any further objections and Piper had to admit it fitted beautifully, as if it had been made for her.

'Then I will be guided by you.' She had no idea what else this evening's dinner party would require, but Elizabeth's air of confidence was reassuring.

'I wish all my clients were so easy to please.' Elizabeth smiled as she signalled to a member of staff that the bronze dress was to be packed. 'Next I have a black gown by the same designer. Perfect for a night at the theatre.'

For a second time Piper looked at her reflection, saw her body encased in the most gorgeous black silk. Was this really happening? The elation of the moment quickly faded as reality crept in. She was paying a high price for this Cinderella moment. She might be about to go to the ball, dinner parties or the theatre, but she certainly wouldn't find her Prince Charming.

From what she'd seen of Dante Mancini, Prince Charming didn't exist in the man she was now engaged to. For two months she'd lived with the hope that after that wonderful night together he might be her very own knight in shining armour. Now she had to accept that such fairytale ideas were impossible. Dante Mancini was ruthless in business and, it seemed, in love. Did he even know what love was?

'No time for daydreaming.' Elizabeth smiled at her in the mirror and Piper couldn't help but smile back, despite the unusual situation and her downward spiralling emotions. 'We have lots more to choose.'

'We do?'

'But of course. You've a weekend in Tuscany, and many events to attend in the coming weeks, and then there are outfits to select for when your pregnancy shows—ones that will accentuate your happy news, as Signor Mancini requested.'

She knew about the pregnancy? Dante certainly hadn't spared her blushes or embarrassment. Hearing it said plainly and so practically that he wanted people knowing that particular detail hurt more than she cared to admit.

'I wasn't aware you knew...' Piper began to stumble over her words, as she always did when she was anxious. 'It's still new to us at the moment.'

Elizabeth stopped and looked at Piper, her friendly

smile defusing the agitation brewing in Piper. 'I'm in full possession of the facts regarding the arrangement between you and Signor Mancini—of his need to appear to settle down in order to salvage the damage done by salacious gossip to their charity.'

'Their charity?'

Piper was confused. Wasn't all this in aid of Dante's business deal? She thought back to the day in his office, when he'd talked of the deal he was on the brink of losing. He hadn't mentioned a charity.

'Of course their charity. That article in *Celebrity Spy!* nearly destroyed the good work all four of them have done.'

'All four of them?'

'Yes—Dante, Zayn, Benjamin and Xander. It's almost as if *Celebrity Spy!* deliberately set out to destroy them and The Hope Foundation.'

Confusion made thinking difficult as Piper digested this new information. Why would Dante want her to believe this was all for his business deal? Why hadn't he told her about the charity, that it was the real reason, instead of letting her believe it was completely mercenary?

'And are all four to be married in order to give the appearance of having settled down in life and abandoned their bachelor existence?'

'Benjamin, Dante and Zayn will be, yes.'

Elizabeth couldn't quite meet Piper's gaze as she straightened a pale pink coat over a dusky pink wrap dress. She wondered where she would wear such an outfit.

'This will be perfect to travel to Tuscany and meet with Dante's clients. Take a look.' Elizabeth's voice held a hint of forced enthusiasm, and she still couldn't meet Piper's eye as she turned to look at her.

Piper walked from the dressing room back to the mirror she'd stood in front of so many times that morning already. The outfit looked and felt expensive, as had each and every one she'd tried on, but it was the turn of the conversation which had unsettled her.

'Are you sure? You seem worried.' Piper's precarious confidence was rocked at the sudden change in Elizabeth's demeanour. She seemed unsettled by the conversation.

'Of course. It's exactly what Dante requested.'

'Dante has mentioned that you arrange marriages. Are you finding brides or inventing fiancées for Benjamin, Zayn and Xander too?'

Piper looked at Elizabeth in the mirror and for a moment thought she saw a look of panic cross her face, but she continued to talk, unable to stop prying into things. This might be her only chance to find out what was really going on, so she continued quickly before Elizabeth changed the subject.

'Each one of them, along with Dante, was named and shamed in that article as the world's most debauched bachelors. Are they *all* your clients?'

'This bag finishes it off perfectly.' Elizabeth handed her a small bag the same colour as the dress and stood and looked at her, a light crease of worry showing on her forehead. 'Benjamin and Zayn are my clients, yes.'

'And is Xander going to follow their lead?' Piper continued to press, aware that maybe Elizabeth shouldn't be divulging such information but, she was part of this charade and had a right to know exactly what was going on. To her, this was for her child, but for Dante their marriage seemed to be about many things—except the duty of fatherhood.

'So I believe.'

'It does make it better, knowing it is also for a charity.' Piper recalled the call she'd interrupted that morning, with Dante unusually speaking English. 'I think Dante did tell you Xander would call you too.'

'Then I shall await his call.' Elizabeth ticked the last item off her list with great flourish. 'We are finished here—but hair, make-up, manicure and pedicure are next.'

'All this for one evening out?'

'You are in a very different world now, Piper. One many women dream of.'

'I'm not one of those women,' she said, and the sensation of losing control of everything, including her destiny, filled her.

CHAPTER FIVE

ELIZABETH'S WORDS HAD stayed with Piper as she'd been made over in a beauty salon. Her nails had been polished and her hair curled until she didn't recognise herself any more. Now as she stood with her hand on the doorhandle of the bedroom, ready to go out and face Dante, wearing a dress that revealed but somehow concealed her body, those words replayed again and again.

She *was* in a different world. One where money bought you anything you desired—including, it seemed, a wife. It didn't help that she wasn't the only woman being groomed for such a role by Elizabeth for the four men in the article. She was acutely aware that she was part of a damage limitation exercise that was more far-reaching than she'd ever thought possible. Worse still, she was his choice only because she carried his child and had come to Rome at precisely the time when he needed a convenient wife.

Piper took a deep breath and looked down at the full-length gown adorned with gold and bronze sequins, wondering if she'd ever truly come up to the standard Dante very obviously desired.

Desired.

That word sizzled in her mind. Last time she'd thrown caution to the wind and worn a gown that wasn't her own she'd ended up in a hotel room with Dante, making passionate love like long-lost lovers who'd been reunited. That night any awkwardness she'd felt about being with him, about giving herself to him, had melted like ice beneath the warmth of spring sunshine as each kiss had pushed her further to the point of no return.

But would he desire her now?

She shook her head, the soft curls making her hair bounce in an unaccustomed way. She couldn't let such thoughts into her mind. This was a deal, not a love affair, and she was adamant she wasn't going to make the same mistake again.

With a determined defiance she opened the door— and the sight which greeted her almost evaporated that self-made promise to ignore the man who made her tremble with just one look. She didn't want to find Dante attractive, but standing in the doorway to his terrace, resplendent in a tuxedo, he took her right back to that night in London. He'd stood out from all the other men that evening—and not just because he'd seemed so captivated by her.

Now he looked even more devastating, and definitely more dangerous than he had then. And he was. He was a danger to her foolish heart, which was thumping so hard in her chest. As he moved towards her his eyes grew dark and intent and swept down her body, making every limb tingle as if he'd actually touched her. And she hated herself for wanting that touch.

'*Mia cara*, you are beautiful.' His voice was rough with desire, and she stood beneath his appraising gaze and knew that every hour she'd spent with Elizabeth and then later in the salon had been worth it. He desired her—even if it was for tonight only.

Right at this moment it was as if the clocks had been

turned back. She felt shy, and yet as completely driven by the sizzle of attraction as she had been that night in London. Just as she had then, she wanted him to take her in his arms and kiss her.

'I trust you are happy with all that Elizabeth has done?' She wouldn't let him know how nice it felt to be told she was beautiful, or how it made her remember things that could never be again. How had he made her feel so desired, so beautiful as they'd made love? Already she knew that moment of passion could never happen again. Not if she wanted to retain her emotional detachment—and her sanity.

'*Sì*, I am very happy, and now I am about to show the beautiful woman who is to be my bride to all of Rome.'

His voice was soft and seductive and it sent a warm tingle sliding down her spine. He took her hand lightly in his fingertips, lifted her fingers to his lips, and without breaking that mesmerising eye contact brushed his lips over them. She wanted to close her eyes as pleasure darted around her. But that would show he affected her, would let him know that he had power over her. Her only weapon in the face of his captivating charm and practised seduction was indifference. She had to remember this was all an act, even if they were not yet in public. It was part of his plan.

'Maybe we should keep the act of being lovers for when we are in the company of tonight's guests.' She forced herself to believe those words but he paused, head bowed slightly over her hand, and raised his brows at her sharp words.

'A man should be able to tell a woman she is beautiful wherever they are.'

There was a playful glint in his eyes and a hint of a mischievous smile. He was toying with her, amusing himself, but it reminded her of his true character. He might be about to fool the rest of the world with his intention to settle down to married life and fatherhood, but she knew the truth—and she had to remember it too.

'Shall we go?' She pulled her hand slowly from his and stepped away from him, needing the space to think, to put her mind back in order. She couldn't fall for his charm—not again. Look what had happened last time the evening had started with a simple kiss of the hand and a seductive smile.

Dante smiled, pleased to know that the act of indifference she'd shown him so far since arriving in Rome was just that. Underneath all that cool composure she was still the hot, sexy woman who had driven him wild with desire. The same one who had lingered in his mind ever since, leaving him with a sense of something unfinished about the whole night.

He'd tried to tell himself it was because she'd left him without even a goodbye, slipping away before dawn, but now he suspected it was a little more than that. For the first time in many years of one-night stands and brief flings he still wanted a woman. More to the point, he wanted *this* woman. The need burned within him to touch her, kiss her and make her his once more.

This insistent need had only been intensified by the attention Elizabeth had given her all day. The bronze dress, alluringly diaphanous, shimmered with bronze and gold sequins which gave the fine fabric its modesty, although it clung to her body as if it had been poured over her. The swell of her breasts which, given the backless design of the dress, had to be braless, was clearly accentuated. As was her slender waist and her hips. The sexy creation hugged her hips, then flared out, but any more detail was lost on him. All he could do was think about her legs and how they had once wrapped around him as he'd thrust into her when he'd been the man to claim her as his—and soon she really would be.

'I have a mind to take you straight back into the bedroom and remove that dress.' He struggled to stabilise his hoarse voice and bit down hard against the rise of hot, throbbing desire which pulsed through him at the thought of doing just that. How had he thought he could keep things neutral with this woman when she'd been in his mind ever since he'd woken to find her gone?

'Is it not suitable?'

Her soft voice wavered anxiously and she brushed those sexy tousled curls back from her face. *Maledizione!* Did she know what she did to him?

She was stunning, beautiful—and the mother of his child. She was now his fiancée. Less than a week ago he had been a single man, a carefree bachelor to whom marriage and commitment had been very much avoidable.

Now he had the responsibility of his child. That thought briefly sobered his desire-infused mind, dredging up his past for inspection once more. He pushed the sabotaging thoughts aside and looked again at the beautiful woman who was to be his wife.

'It has achieved all that I hoped for, *cara*, and I am certain that I will not be the only man to want to do just that this evening.' His voice remained hoarse with desire, just as desire lingered in his body, not quite extinguished.

As she frowned in confusion he crossed the room to her, unable to resist the urge to touch her, to feel her soft skin beneath his fingers, his lips. *Dio mio*, he wanted her more than he'd ever wanted any woman—even more than he'd wanted her that first night in London.

He saw the moment she realised his intention, saw her step back, saw the blush spread over her face and it made him want her more. He'd never been so hungry for a woman and he'd never had to control such desires. He was used to getting what he wanted, and right now he wanted this Australian redhead—badly.

'No.' That sharp, short word cracked through the sexually charged air and she stood in glorious defiance, her chin lifted, her shoulders back and those lovely green eyes sparking icy fury at him. 'We made a deal, Dante, one that doesn't include such things. We are not a real couple.'

'*Sì, cara*, you are right. *Mi dispiace.*' English mixed with his native Italian as he fought for control over his response to seeing her like this.

One thing it did prove was that she was definitely unfinished business. Would the deal he'd struck with her be enough to keep him at a distance? It should be—as should the fact that he never wanted to care for anyone again, never wanted to be responsible for another person's happiness. He was done with caring, done with losing a piece of himself when a person left, and Piper had made it clear that she intended to leave once the minimum term of their marriage had been completed, taking with her his child. No, he mustn't allow emotions to cloud this deal.

'Just as long as we understand one another.'

Her deep and fast breathing told him she was far from unaffected by what had almost happened, even if her words were cold and to the point. She might not want to be his wife, but she wanted him as much as he wanted her.

'Very clearly, *cara*, and now we should go. I have timed our arrival to create maximum impact and so begin the talk of our engagement within the media.'

She looked down at the ring on her finger, her curled hair sliding off her shoulder in a way that was so sensual it almost undid all the control he'd fought hard to regain. He knew what she was thinking as she looked at the symbol of their deal. The platinum band set with a single large diamond would certainly be noticed. There would be no doubt that they were engaged.

'Yes, you're right,' she said, with a new strength sounding in her voice. 'The sooner you achieve your aims, the sooner we can return to something resembling normal. I can go back to London and you can continue as if this never happened.'

'That may not be possible for a while. It is going to be hard to prove to Bettino D'Antonio that I have reformed my ways without you at my side, but there is time later to discuss this—the car is waiting.' The thought of her returning to London so soon unsettled him, but he wasn't ready to explore why.

All too soon they were ensconced in the elevator, and her perfume brought back memories of that morning at his office a few days earlier. Then he had thought his imagination was playing tricks on him when the lingering scent in the elevator had brought her so quickly to his mind. The scent was evocative of that night in London, of the passion they'd shared, and now as they got into the car it reminded him far more than he could tolerate.

He studied her as she sat, determinedly staring forward while the car made its way through Rome's traffic, and wondered if she too felt the zing of electricity which connected them, gaining strength each day.

'Goodness,' she gasped and looked at him, her green eyes vivid and wide. 'So many cameras. I don't think I can do this.'

He took her hand and looked into the depths of green which reminded him of the forests of Italy in summer. 'You can. I'm with you.'

Her gaze held his and the connection between them intensified, sending off sparks around them. He had to kiss her—had to feel her lips beneath his and the soft swell of her breasts against his chest as he held her. He had to wrap his arms around her and feel her pliant body melt against his. He couldn't resist her any longer.

He leant closer. She didn't pull away, didn't move back, and her eyes darkened until they resembled the deepest ocean. She wanted him too. Despite the icy indifference she was hiding behind, she wanted him. A pulse of lust hurtled through him as she nervously moistened her lips with her tongue, the movement taking his gaze from those dark desire-filled eyes. *She wanted him.*

'I can't do any of this…' Piper whispered as Dante leant closer. He was going to kiss her. Instinctively she recognised the inky blackness which had filled his eyes, obliterating the brown completely, and she was powerless to resist. She couldn't move—couldn't do anything except wait to feel his lips on hers and hate herself for wanting that kiss, *needing* it.

He whispered something so seductive-sounding it could only be Italian, and she closed her eyes as his lips touched hers, sending shockwaves of tingles throughout her body. Then his hands held her face, imprisoning her as he pressed a deep and scorching kiss to her lips. She sighed softly when hot desire sparked to life within her, just as it had that night in London—as if nothing had changed. She sighed again and responded, and her breathing quickened as the kiss deepened.

What was she doing?

'No.' She pushed against him, her breath coming hard and fast. Every nerve in her body sang with awareness for him but she couldn't let it happen again, couldn't give in to it. 'I can't.'

He smiled at her, so sure of himself, completely convinced that just one kiss would have her tumbling back into his bed. 'You just did, *cara*.'

'I don't mean *that*.' She adopted a dismissive tone, as if being kissed to within an inch of her sanity was a perfectly normal occurrence. 'I mean all those photographers out there. I can't be who you want me to be.'

'You can and you will. We have a deal, no?'

His eyes narrowed and she looked out of the window, not relishing the idea of parading around for what appeared to be nothing short of a pack of wolves in such a tight dress when her body was on fire from his kiss.

'What if I get it wrong?' She turned and looked at him to see his brows rise in question. Then he smiled and her attention was drawn to that smile, to those lips which had just kissed her into a heady state of euphoria. She couldn't allow that again and would have to be on her guard.

'Do not worry, *mia cara*, I will be at your side all the way.'

That was precisely what she was worried about. But as she got out of the car and the cameras flashed Dante was true to his word and stayed at her side, the act of loving fiancé in full swing.

She smiled shyly as they stood briefly for photos and Dante put his arm around her, his fingers pressing possessively into her waist as he pulled her closer, giving her no option but to lean against the length of his body. The spark of desire which had just been reawakened hummed relentlessly through her until it was almost impossible to smile at the cameras.

If she'd thought the kiss had been potent then she'd definitely got it wrong. It was as if she was going up in flames of desire right there on the streets of Rome. His masculine and powerful musky aftershave weaved its way through her senses and the firmness of his thigh against hers brought images to her mind of them naked together.

Then Dante spoke to the press, turning her towards the hotel as he did so, and she focused all her attention on walking the short distance in heels she was far from used to. Anything was better than focusing on the feel of his body against hers and the heady pulse of desire which beat within her.

'Is it always like this?' she asked as they entered the peace and safety of the hotel.

'You will get used to it.'

He guided her through to the function room, where tables were laid with precise attention to detail. At least that was *something* she was familiar with after spending so many hours setting such tables and waiting on them as the rich and famous of first Sydney and then London dined while she remained invisible. She wholeheartedly wished she could do that right now—but dressed as she was, with a man like Dante at her side and desire coursing within her, that wasn't an option.

'I'm not sure I want to.' She was painfully aware of the curious glances and bold stares and didn't like it at all. It played too much into her insecurities, reminding her of childhood taunts.

'That sounds distinctly like you want to back out of our deal, Piper.' He took two flutes of champagne and handed her one, but she shook her head in refusal and instantly he sent for a more suitable drink.

'I'm not backing out of anything,' she said with a smile on her lips and a sweetness in her voice that she hoped would convey her annoyance. 'I'm going through with this deal for the right reason.'

'Which is…?'

How could he even ask that?

She paused as a waiter approached with a single glass of juice on a silver tray. Dante took it with thanks and handed it to her.

She looked straight into those sinfully dark eyes. 'Our child.'

'And I am not?' How could he boldly stand there and say that when he'd been the one to make such a deal?

'No, you are doing this for a business deal—although you'd like everyone to think it's for a charitable reason. But if there is one thing I know about you now, it is that you couldn't possibly want to marry—even for your child. Everything I read about you in *Celebrity Spy!* is true. So far I have found nothing to make me think otherwise.'

'At least you are well informed about me, whereas I know very little of you.'

She bristled as the conversation turned in a way she hadn't expected. 'There isn't much to tell.'

'I'd like to know why you were the hostess at that dinner party in London—"stepping in", I think you called it. What exactly *is* your profession?'

She tried to suppress the urge to shock him, but it was too great. 'I'm just a waitress.' It wasn't her choice of job—wasn't what she'd hoped for as she'd started university in Australia—but circumstances had conspired against her.

She watched as he clenched his jaw and a surge of triumph rushed through her. He had certainly never envisaged marriage and fatherhood, and she was completely sure that if he had he wouldn't have wanted his wife to be a mere waitress.

'And that is enough for you?'

'It's had to be,' she said, without realising she was opening the door to a discussion about herself she'd rather not have. She didn't want to talk about her beloved father, about the emptiness in her life where he had been. She was an ordinary girl—but to her father she'd been a princess, and he'd been the most important person in her life.

Thankfully at that very moment other guests joined them, and after that there wasn't much chance to talk— at least not about anything private, and especially not her past, nor the events which had changed her life. That was something she had no wish to share with a man incapable of any kind of emotion. He would never understand.

Dante unlocked the door to his apartment and for the first time since he'd been relegated to the small room which usually served as his home office he was glad of it. At least there he would be away from the temptation to kiss Piper, because after spending the evening being tormented by her body in the bronze creation Elizabeth had selected he was in danger of giving in to the lustful desire which pumped through him.

Never before had he had to restrain himself. He *always* got what he wanted, be it women or fast cars.

Holding back was not a comfortable sensation, and he didn't know how long he could go on being tempted so enticingly by her without acting on it.

'Piper…' He spoke softly as she placed her purse on the antique table in the living area. He wanted to tell her again how lovely she looked, and how much he wanted her, but instead decided that keeping to the terms of their agreement was better—for both of them. He couldn't allow himself to care, knowing she would one day walk away. Just as she had done the night after his baby had been conceived.

She looked at him, her big green eyes full of uncertainty, and when she bit her lower lip he clenched his hands into fists at his sides. Now was not the time to remember how those lips had felt beneath his just hours earlier, how they'd responded so willingly. Nor was it the time to remember that if they had been here instead of in the car when he'd kissed her they would never have left for the dinner party.

'Is something wrong?' she asked tentatively.

Everything was wrong. He was falling under a spell he was beginning to think she had no idea she was casting. She seemed oblivious to what she did to him. Tonight he'd seen her smile and laugh with people she didn't know, seen them warm to her in a way which had made pride fill him as she visibly blossomed.

'I just wanted to say you made a good impression this evening. Thank you.'

'I did it for my baby.'

She flung the words at him instantly and he bit back his retort. It was late, and now was not the time to be getting embroiled in a discussion he didn't want, no matter what the time of day. The way she'd said *my baby* cut deep into his hardened emotions, more pain-fully than he'd thought possible.

'Tomorrow we will be leaving for Tuscany, where you will do it all again—this time for me and my deal.'

CHAPTER SIX

PIPER SAT IN the sports car as it sped along the road towards Tuscany, glad that the threat of morning sickness she'd experienced earlier in the week seemed to have dwindled. Beside her Dante drove with clean precision, and she couldn't help but glance at him as he drove, embarrassed when he caught her out. His sunglasses hid the truth in his eyes and probably, after the burning look of desire he'd had in them when they'd returned from the dinner party last night, that was for the best.

She had no wish to fall even harder for him than she had already, and certainly didn't want to repeat their encounter in London. This was all about their child. Nothing else mattered other than giving her son or daughter the experience of knowing both parents.

'We are almost there,' he said, and quickly looked at her. 'Tonight we dine with Bettino D'Antonio at his new villa, so it would be best if we exchanged a few details about each other before this evening, no?'

'Is that in the interests of making our engagement believable or out of a genuine need to know more about the mother of your child?' He'd caught her off-guard with his callous disregard for her feelings and she'd risen to the challenge he'd inadvertently given. They would never be a real couple, but he would always be her child's father, and she intended to remind him of that duty as often as possible.

'Such attention to detail is necessary whatever the reason.' He slowed the car and turned off the main road onto a narrower road which twisted through a small and sleepy village before heading out into the countryside once more. 'This weekend will be make or break after months of negotiations between myself and D'Antonio. He has also invited Gianni Paolini, my rival in this deal, so I fully intend to use our newly announced engagement and the baby to maximum benefit.'

The tension of several hours in the car with Dante, being excruciatingly aware of every move he made, got the better of her and she couldn't help but continue to aim for irritation. 'And by that you mean I shouldn't elaborate on what I know about you, but paint a very different picture?'

'It is what we agreed, Piper.'

He swung the car into a driveway lined with mature cypress trees and, knowing he was right, she looked away just in time to see a large villa come into view.

'That's so beautiful…' she breathed, more to herself than to Dante.

'It pleases me to hear you say that,' he said as he stopped the car outside the old stone villa. 'This is where I come to get away from everything. Except for this weekend, it is the one place I am able to completely relax. Bettino D'Antonio has recently bought a villa in the next village, which he intends to use during the winter months, and despite the fact I'd rather not conduct business from here, it suits me well.'

Dante got out of the car and she watched him walk around the front of its sleek black bonnet. He looked up at the villa as he did so and briefly she thought she saw his face relax, as if this was a place where he truly was at home.

When he opened her door she slid round in the seat and tried to get out in as elegant a fashion as the tight-fitting skirt would allow. She failed miserably, if the raising of his brows was anything to go by, as her skirt rucked up, exposing her legs. With a wicked and suggestive expression on his face he held out his hand to her and helped her out of the low car.

'I have arranged for lunch to be served on the terrace. We can talk further on things we should know about each other, and after that you should rest before this evening's dinner.'

Piper didn't know if she wanted to talk to Dante at all. She had no wish to share her past with a man who cared for nothing other than getting the next deal. But if he *did* get that deal she would have honoured her side of their bargain. Would he then keep *his* promise and be there for his child? She was in no doubt that her son or daughter would not have the kind of relationship she'd had with her own father—the kind that had driven her to board a plane for Rome, convinced she was doing the right thing to seek Dante out. She hadn't wanted to deny her child the chance to have what she'd had, but as each day passed she was more certain than ever that Dante was nothing like her father.

'If we are going to convince people that we are engaged for real then I suppose we do have to at least know a little of each other.'

She followed him into the villa, taking in the luxurious interior. It looked far more like a home than the sleek modern style of his Rome apartment, and her curiosity was aroused by the paintings and antiques she glimpsed.

Dante opened two doors which led out onto a terrace covered in wisteria that would be beautiful in the summer. 'We *are* engaged for real, no?'

The tone of his voice left her in no doubt that he was taunting her—and enjoying it.

No, they weren't. If it was for real she would be helplessly in love with him, and he would definitely be in love with her. She couldn't deny there was an attraction, but it wasn't love. Was it?

'Not in the true sense of the word, no. We are not in love.'

'But to look as if we are in love is what we have agreed on, *cara*, is it not?'

'For very different reasons, yes, it is.'

'Then I suggest we relax and enjoy our meal and the winter sunshine Tuscany has to offer before making sure it does appear to anyone we meet that ours is very much a real engagement.'

He sat at the table, looking far too relaxed and comfortable with the whole situation, whereas she was nothing but jumbled nerves. Was that the deal she'd struck with Dante, or the man himself? She couldn't even consider the answer to that question.

'You look tired,' Dante said as he sat back.

The sought-after calm that usually settled over him after arriving in Tuscany wasn't quite so easy to come by today, but then he'd never been here to do business before—and that business had never been so important or so wanted. He *had* to win this contract, and it was that sentiment, together with the way the charity would view him, that had forced him to accept that Benjamin's suggestion of settling down was the answer to many issues—including, it seemed, a night of amazing but careless sex with a gorgeous redhead he hadn't even bothered exchanging names with.

'I am a little tired. Can we sort these things out now, so I can rest before taking a shower?' She pushed her hair behind her ear and looked at him, the vivid green of her eyes holding a hint of unease.

He pushed aside the guilt that he was making her uncomfortable and tried to banish the image which had suddenly sprung to mind of her in the shower. It wouldn't do to think of her naked beneath jets of water—not when he knew just how amazing she looked naked.

'When and where we met will remain the same—at least there is little chance of getting that wrong. However, we will say we have been seeing each other secretly since.' Briskness crept into his voice as he set out all that was supposed to have happened between them.

'Why secretly?' Her delicate brows furrowed in genuine confusion, making her look every bit as innocent as she had been—unknown to him—before he took her to his hotel room in London.

'To protect you from press attention, of course—except that it didn't go according to plan, as the *Celebrity Spy!* article will prove, giving me the perfect opportunity to refute its claims.'

'And where will these meetings have taken place?' She spoke in an efficient manner and might have been conducting a business meeting.

'London and Rome. What do you like doing? Where would you have wanted to go?

She looked at him, the hardness in her eyes softening slightly. 'Art galleries.'

'Art? I had no idea.' He was genuinely surprised, but couldn't allow himself to get sidetracked now.

'Why should you have? Neither of us expected the night we shared to become anything more than one night. We didn't even exchange names.'

She strolled across the terrace, folding her arms about her as if trying to keep every detail about herself protected from him. He watched as she stood and looked out across the rise and fall of the landscape he loved so much, interspersed as it was by clusters of ancient villages.

He hadn't expected anything from those few hot hours in bed with her, and certainly not to wake up alone the next morning. Was that why she'd lingered in his mind, teasing his memory with the passion of that night? Now, as he watched her, his gaze taking in her petite and slender figure showcased to perfection in another creation suggested by Elizabeth, he really did want to know more about her. What did she like? What was her favourite music and food? Questions raced through his mind.

'And what of your family?' He had to know at least something of her family background.

'My family?' She looked at him, suspicion in her eyes. 'It is just my mother and myself. We moved to London, her place of birth, after my father died.'

A jolt of something akin to sympathy raced through him. She knew what it was to lose someone she loved too.

'But you grew up in Australia?' He walked over to her, conscious of her watching him carefully, keeping her attention fully focused on him, just as she had done that first morning in his office.

'Yes, in Sydney. Anything else about my childhood you feel it's necessary to know?'

The scathing tone of her voice should have warned

him off, but knowing she too had lost her father drew him to her, as did a strange urge to talk of something he'd long since buried.

'You at least knew your father, had a bond with him, which is more than I ever experienced.'

'I'm sorry.' The sympathetic look in her eyes as she looked up at him, placing her hand on his arm, conveyed her shock at the unexpected revelation which had come from him.

'Don't be.' He shrugged off her touch and focused his gaze into the Tuscan countryside. 'I barely knew my father, which is just as well. He wasn't a man I would have wished to know.'

'Don't say that.' Her shock rushed over him in waves. 'Every child needs a father.'

'Not one who walks out on a woman, a young boy and a newborn son. No child deserves a father like *that*.'

'That happened to you?' Her gorgeous green eyes were filled with sympathy and he gritted his teeth against it. He didn't need sympathy from anyone— least of all her.

'*Sì.*' His overpowering anger made functioning in English briefly impossible.

'Where is your brother now?'

Piper's question rocked him to the core as memories of the time when that had been the only question he'd wanted an answer to flooded back faster than a high tide.

'He died.' The hounds were after him again, dragging out the horror of those years when he and his mother had had no idea where the teenage Alessio had gone. He couldn't do this now. He didn't want to share any of this with anyone, and definitely not a fiancée acquired through a deal. 'He was missing for several years before I discovered the truth of his untimely death.'

'That makes all *I* went through as a child seem so trivial.'

He turned to her just as she looked down, as if ashamed of even admitting such a thing. 'What *did* you go through?'

She still didn't look at him. 'I was born without sight in my left eye, and before I had an operation to make it look normal I was teased mercilessly by other children. Then I was knocked down by a car when I was seven. I didn't see the car, which thankfully wasn't going fast, but after that my parents—especially my father—wrapped me up and tried to keep me from all harm. I just wish I could have done the same for Dad. Maybe then he wouldn't have been killed when a car he was a passenger in crashed.'

Before Dante could think what he was doing he'd taken Piper in his arms and hugged her. Her willing body moulded against him and he stroked her hair, inhaling the scent of her shampoo, wanting only to make her pain go away.

'I had no idea,' he said, thinking again of what she had first said, and the way she always kept her focus on him, especially in his office that first morning. It made sense now.

'I don't like to talk of my father.' She looked up at him and he studied her closely.

'I meant about your sight.'

Before she could drop her gaze he caught her chin with his thumb and finger, forcing her to look at him. 'Nobody would ever know.'

She pulled away from him, a flush of embarrassment

colouring her cheeks. 'We can talk more later. I'm not feeling too good.'

He watched her go, wanting to call her back, to hold her to him again and give her comfort. Because, strangely, just having her in his arms gave *him* comfort. It was a sensation he was not at all sure about and so, feeling like a child learning to swim, enjoying the warm water and yet finding it terrifying, he moved swiftly to the water's edge and out of danger. Sentiment was something he'd never dabbled with, and now was not the time to start.

Piper's nerves were almost frayed as she and Dante entered the villa of the man he wanted to do business with—the man *she* had to convince their relationship was real.

She'd put on the emerald-green dress that Elizabeth had selected for the dinner, still ruffled by the fact that Elizabeth had known more of what was expected of her than Piper had. But that indignation had melted away when Dante had first seen her, looking at her not with the scrutiny she'd expected, but with genuine pleasure. And if she wasn't mistaken there had also been a hint of something else which had sent a shiver of anticipation through her...

But now was not the time, and she focused herself. She had a role to play—her part of the deal they'd struck a week ago in Rome.

'Dante,' Bettino said as he met them, taking Dante's hand and shaking it firmly. 'I confess that I was sceptical about the news that you had become engaged, but now I can see exactly why a man such as yourself would succumb to the need for marriage.'

Piper smiled graciously at Bettino and tried to ignore

the frisson of tension which had transferred itself from Dante to her at the other man's words.

'Bettino, meet Piper Riley—my fiancée.' Remarkably Dante supressed the tension and pride shone out in his voice. Piper felt her stomach flip over with nerves, still unable to believe she'd actually agreed to this charade.

She wanted to shy away from Bettino, despite his friendly smile and grandfather-like eyes. All she wanted to do was step back from his scrutiny and the limelight to a place where she felt safe, but this was part of the deal she'd made with Dante and she would do it so well even *he* wouldn't question her authenticity. She had to if she stood a chance of Dante being any kind of father to their child.

She smiled at the man Dante wanted to secure his deal with and harnessed all she'd been told about being in the public eye—first by the company she'd worked for in Sydney and then in London, and finally by Elizabeth, who had instructed her in the art of being the kind of woman a man like Dante would need at his side.

'Thank you for inviting me to your lovely home, Signor D'Antonio. It's a real pleasure to be here with Dante.'

As she spoke Dante slid his arm around her back and she breathed in slowly against the heat his touch sent scorching through her. She glanced up at him, thankful he'd at least stayed on her right side so she hadn't jumped when he'd touched her. Maybe telling him about her lack of sight hadn't been such a bad idea. Even if it *had* come out before she'd been able to stop it—something which never normally happened.

'I am pleased Dante has brought you. It is always a pleasure to meet a beautiful woman.'

'The pleasure is, of course, all mine, Bettino.' Dante's voice positively dripped with desire and admiration as he looked down at her, and the smile on his lips would have fooled anyone. As would the soft, desire-laden darkness of his eyes.

'My other guests will arrive shortly,' Bettino said, turning his attention back to Dante. 'And after this evening I will make my decision as to whom I do business with. But for now I want you both to relax and enjoy the evening. I want to see the real Dante Mancini, just as I want to see the real Gianni Paolini.'

'A very astute way of doing business,' Dante said, and Piper wondered if it was only her who noticed his jaws pressing tightly together.

Bettino laughed and they followed him into the villa, where they were offered a glass of champagne by a waitress—a role Piper felt far more suited to.

'Piper would prefer juice,' Dante said, and pulled her close again, looking down at her. 'We're looking forward to being parents.'

Bettino laughed and clapped a hand on Dante's shoulder. 'So not only are you to be married, but you are to be a father too?'

Piper blushed furiously at Dante's not so subtle way of informing Bettino of their news, but all thought was swept away as Gianni Paolini arrived with his wife.

He was an older Italian man who was nearer Bettino's age. Beside her she felt Dante's presence, and that unmistakable aura of power he'd had on the night they'd met in London. But would it be enough? Suddenly it mattered to her.

As the meal began the men talked around the subject of the deal, and Piper listened as Dante spoke passionately about his business. Her interest was aroused when

Bettino asked him why he'd started his own business, and she watched as he seemed to square his shoulders.

'I started as a teenager, clearing building sites of off-cuts and soon it became a large and expanding company—one which I hoped would make things better for my mother, who'd brought me and my brother up alone.'

'You have a brother?' Bettino asked, and Piper held her breath, hardly hearing the meaningless talk of the other women.

'My brother died.' Silence hung in the air, suspended on an atmosphere that might have been sliced with one swipe of a sword.

Thankfully the two older women had begun to talk about the various regions of Tuscany and Piper joined in, eager to divert attention from Dante. 'There are many parts of Tuscany I'd love to see.'

'Then you must ask your fiancé to take you,' said Gianni Paolini's wife.

Piper thought her tactics had worked—until suddenly and inexplicably the spotlight was turned on her.

'What do *you* do, Piper?' Bettino's wife asked.

Piper felt as if she was about to be tripped up, tricked into saying she was just a waitress—an unemployed one at that. Determined not to be outwitted, she drew on her career dreams. 'Art is my passion. I studied it at university for a time.'

'You didn't finish your course?' The question, full of conjecture, hung in the air, and to make matters worse she could feel Dante's gaze on her now.

'No, I didn't. I moved home to be with my parents when my father became very ill.' Saying it aloud brought all the pain back.

'What would you have done with your degree in art?' In stark contrast to his wife, Bettino's voice was full of interest and, as always, she blossomed beneath such genuine interest in her subject.

'I would have set up my own business as an art curator.' She pushed back the agony of losing her father and focused on the one thing she'd always been passionate about. Art.

Bettino sat back and looked at her as their main course arrived. 'We should talk later. I am looking to commission someone to bring this place to life with art.'

'Thank you, but I couldn't—not with a baby due in the summer.'

'Nonsense.' Bettino's voice softened. 'We'll sort something out.'

Piper almost couldn't keep the fizz of excitement at such a prospect under control, but she had to. She had to remember this was Dante's deal, not hers. With a smile she was unable to hide she looked across the table at him, and the irritation or annoyance she'd thought would be there after that little exchange was missing. In its place she saw the same desire he'd had in his eyes as they'd arrived, but somehow it was more intense. It seemed to smoulder, and she could feel the heat across the table.

She blushed and looked down, hoping the conversation would take a different turn.

'Do you plan to spend a lot of time here?' Dante asked Bettino, and Piper wondered if that had been a deliberate ploy to rescue her. Whatever it was, she was glad that she was no longer the centre of attention.

As the hour moved towards midnight Dante placed Piper's coat over her shoulders, pleased the evening had gone well. Piper had been amazing—she'd become the confident and vivacious woman he'd met in London.

She'd held her own as they'd asked her questions which, from their earlier talk, he knew would cause her pain. He'd found himself drawn to her in a way he'd never known, eager to discover more of the woman beneath the sexy exterior, but he'd quickly dismissed that idea.

That night they'd first met in London he'd experienced mind-blowing sex with her, unwittingly taking her virginity and creating a child that would bind them together for ever. But that didn't alter anything. No matter where she was or who she was with she would always be his, and even though he didn't want to tonight he would have to watch her close the door to her bedroom and shut him out.

It was for the best. He didn't want commitment and emotion. It was something he couldn't do, because the few times in his life that he had, it had forced away those he'd invested in emotionally, locking them out of his life for ever. He'd sworn after Alessio's death never to become emotionally involved with anyone ever again.

But with Piper that pledge was difficult to keep. She entranced him, made him desire her with just one of those coy looks she often gave him when she thought he wasn't looking. When she'd admitted her lack of sight in her left eye he'd wanted to hold her and show that it made no difference to him at all, that she was the most desirable and sexy woman he'd ever known. He wanted more than ever to care for her, protect her always.

After the way she'd had Bettino D'Antonio practically eating out of her hand he wanted her even more. She'd been marvellous tonight, her beauty subtly shinning in a way that the vain women he usually dated could never have achieved. It had made him want her again, in his arms and in his bed. Before their marriage ended and they went their separate ways he wanted her—completely.

He lowered his head to her left ear, about to whisper how well she'd done, when she jumped and turned abruptly to face him, a spark of annoyance in her green eyes. It quickly faded as she remembered her role and she smiled sweetly at him just as Bettino joined them in the large hallway. He berated himself for not remembering what she'd told him earlier, but the need to be close to her had become overwhelming, just as it had that night in London when nothing else had mattered except making her his.

'You startled me,' she said softly, before looking again at Bettino. 'Thank you again for such an interesting evening, and I'd be honoured to help you locate any items of art you require.'

'Thank you. I will definitely contact you regarding this matter,' Bettino stated firmly, and for a moment Dante wondered what was coming next.

Had something been said or done this evening to jeopardise the deal? He'd thought Piper's love of art might have clinched the deal, maybe forcing the older man to make up his mind before the end of the evening.

The genuine look of shocked joy on Piper's face at Bettino's words was so unexpected that Dante laughed gently at her innocent pleasure.

'I will wait to hear from you, *signor*,' she said.

'Goodnight, Mancini,' said Bettino as Dante put his arm possessively around Piper—not for show, as he expected she thought it might be, but because he wanted to.

He needed to feel her close, to inhale the heady scent of her perfume and feel that gorgeous body next to his. The thought of saying goodnight to her once they returned to his villa was not one he welcomed—not when the insistent throb of desire was alive in his body. He wanted her more than he'd ever wanted any woman.

'Goodnight, Signor D'Antonio.'

Bettino turned to Piper and took her hand, bowing over it as if he would kiss it in a gesture suited to another century, sending a spark of jealousy hurtling through Dante as she blushed and smiled shyly at him.

'Goodnight, Piper. I'm very pleased to have made your acquaintance. Your presence here this evening has been most welcome.'

'Thank you,' Piper said softly, sending a thrill of desire sparking through Dante.

She was a beautiful woman, inside and out, and a woman like that wasn't right for him. But that knowledge didn't curb the need which was pulsing through him.

That need and desire, which he doubted he could suppress for much longer, formed a potent cocktail as he drove as fast as the narrow roads would allow back to his villa, aware of her watching his every move in a way which added to the sexual tension swirling around them.

Did she feel it too?

There was no way out of it now—no way of avoiding it. He wanted Piper and he wanted her tonight. *Now*.

CHAPTER SEVEN

PIPER WATCHED DANTE as he strode across the high-ceil-inged living room of the villa. The look on his face was intense her heart beat a little faster. He looked as if he wanted to devour her there and then. The same expression he'd had as they'd entered his hotel room in London.

'You made a good impression this evening.' He stopped striding and stood, leaning one arm along the cream stone of the fireplace, and she fought hard against the dark and passionate look which filled his eyes—and the way her body responded.

She couldn't want him—not after he'd shown his true colours, shown himself to be a sharp and driven businessman who would stop at nothing to achieve his ultimate aims. He was using her and their baby. How could she find such a man attractive when all she'd ever dreamed of was a caring, loving man? He was so wrong for her, and yet being with him felt so right. Just as be-fore, she wanted to be with him in every way possible, to risk everything and feel his kiss, his touch.

She certainly hadn't been fooled by his subdued and grief-laden voice as he'd spoken of his brother at the dinner table. He'd spoken of how difficult things had been for his mother, bringing up two young boys. Such a revelation had come as a shock, but she hoped she'd hidden it well. After all, as his fiancée she would have known such things.

'I did my best,' she said now, and sat down on one of the large, comfortable sofas. She couldn't stay in the middle of the room, watching him as if she were waiting for something to happen. She was certain that at any moment the tension around them would snap.

'You were utterly brilliant and you won D'Antonio over. He loved you. He practically melted each time you spoke and you know it.'

There was a caustic edge to his words as they sliced through the atmosphere in the room and she knew right there and then that something had changed. It felt different between them, and she didn't know what it was.

'Telling him of your passion for art was a clever move.'

'It is real, Dante. It is what I would have done if I hadn't given up university when my father became ill.'

'A well-played move, no?'

'I should go to bed.' She got up. The need to escape both the brooding man who dominated every bit of space in the room and the way her body yearned for his touch and his kiss was overwhelming. She definitely had to go.

'Tell me about your father's illness.'

Dante's words froze her to the spot and she looked at him, still standing without a care in the world, so casually leaning on the mantelpiece of the fireplace.

'There's nothing more to tell.' She fired the words defensively back at him as grief assailed her, rushing back so strongly her legs felt weak. She wanted to sit down, but doing so would mean staying beneath his scrutiny.

'It would have helped me to know of such a detail

before spending the evening with D'Antonio, trying to convince him we are a couple in love—a couple about to marry and share our lives—which means sharing our pasts.'

'That's something you too are guilty of.'

He pushed firmly away from the fireplace and came towards her, but she couldn't move, even though she knew she should. The fierce intensity in his eyes struck fear into her heart, closely followed by anticipation. For what, she didn't know.

'But we are not really sharing our lives, are we, Dante? We are engaged to be married, and it is merely for the convenience of your business deal.'

Now all the worries she'd had about the future over the last week pushed forth and she couldn't stem the flow of words.

'What will happen when you get your stupid deal? Will you walk away from me, from your child, as if we never existed?'

Dante closed the distance between them, coming to stand very close to her, making her heart pound in a way she'd only experienced once before, on the night he took her hand and led her to his hotel room.

'You don't think very highly of me, do you, *cara*?'

He spoke softly, serving only to irritate her further. She wasn't a sullen child to be appeased.

'Your reputation isn't exactly squeaky clean, Dante. What am I supposed to think?'

She wasn't about to stand there and discuss this tonight, least of all admit how much she liked him—and more. She was tired—which, together with the pregnancy, must be the reason for her emotions being all over the place. It couldn't be Dante. She didn't want it to be Dante—didn't want him to affect her.

'I never go back on a deal, Piper. *Ever.*' A firm and sharp edge speared into his words, and if they'd been discussing anything else she might just have fallen for it. 'I needed to know about your father's illness. It's the sort of detail a loving fiancé *would* know.'

'Very well.' She flounced away from him, desperate to reinstate the distance between them. She couldn't deal with the scent of his aftershave invading her senses, the heat of his body so very close to hers, and definitely not his dark penetrating gaze, watching her so intently. 'What do you need to know?'

'When did he die?'

Piper closed her eyes briefly and took a deep breath, not sure she could do this now, but acutely aware that what he said made sense. If they were to look like a newly engaged couple he had to know at least *something* about her.

'The night I met you in London was the first anniversary of his death.' She lifted her chin and looked into his eyes, unwittingly sending him a challenge to ask more. A challenge he took.

'So you used the attraction between us as a way to escape?' He visibly stiffened before her, his whole body becoming rigid and his dark eyes almost fusing her to the spot.

'Yes,' she stated boldly, still ashamed at the way she'd needed to rebel against everything she'd stood for, every moral she'd been brought up to believe in. The only problem now was that she could see why her mother had insisted they both move to London. To keep what little of her family she had left together. Wasn't she herself about to throw her life into this man's hands for the sake of her unborn child?

'Why me? Had you planned this outcome all along? This unexpected pregnancy?'

He flung his hands up in a gesture of frustration and turned away from her, giving her time to recover. But any recovery was short-lived. The next time he looked at her angry sparks glittered in his eyes.

'Was that why you didn't insist on contraception?'

'No!' she gasped, and stepped back away from his anger. 'I thought you were telling me it was taken care of.'

He moved towards her and she took another step back until she met the coolness of the wall behind her, finding strength in it.

'Did you perhaps know who I was that night?'

'I had no idea who you were, and if I had I would never, ever have left the party with you.' Angered by her silly notions of fate having brought them together, on that night of all nights, she met his fury head-on. 'I can't do this any more.'

He moved menacingly closer. 'What can't you do?'

His voice had deepened, his accent heightened, and the look in his dark eyes of anger blending with veiled passion made her heart thump so hard it almost hurt.

'This pretence,' she flung at him, unable to unlock her gaze from his or stop the pounding of her heart.

'And what pretence would that be, *cara*?'

'The…the engagement.' She stammered the words out as he moved a little closer, those sexy eyes looking deep into her soul, as if finding the answer she couldn't even give herself.

'I think you mean the cold indifference you have adopted since you arrived in Rome.'

'It is the only way to get through this charade.' She hated it that her voice gave her away and turned into a whisper, that his close proximity was starving her of the last remnants of stamina and strength she had left after the last few hours.

'But it is *not* all a charade—is it, *mia cara*?'

He touched her face, the contact of his fingers on her skin so soft, but she couldn't stop the deep breath being dragged from her. And she hated the satisfaction which played on his lips and sparked in his eyes. She hated him and yet she wanted him. Badly.

'Of course it is.' Her breathing was impossible to control and she drew it in deep and hard as he looked down to her neck, where he must surely see her pulse beating wildly, and then to her breasts, which rose and fell with each deep breath. 'You mean nothing to me.'

'Don't lie.'

The intensity in his eyes sent a spiral of hot need flooding down through her, right to the very heart of her femininity.

'Or I may have to prove you wrong…prove how untrue that is.'

'Don't you dare!' she gasped in shock, while inside a traitorous voice called, *I dare you to.*

The glint in his eyes fired with desire and she knew exactly what he was going to do. He was going to kiss her—and she wanted him to. She wanted to feel his lips on hers, to taste him and so much more. But that wasn't the deal they'd made. The deal they'd made had been on paper only, was one that meant they would have nothing physical to do with each other and certainly nothing emotional.

'Never challenge me, Piper. I always accept—and I always win.'

'Not this time.' She glared up at him, more angry

at her own reaction to him than at his boast of always winning.

'So…' His brows rose suggestively and he placed the palm of one hand on the wall, leaning over her so that his face was so close she only needed to lift her chin and her lips would find his. 'The challenge still stands, no?'

'No…' She dragged the hoarse whisper out, hoping for resolve but knowing she sounded more as if she'd dissolved.

'And if I kiss you will it do nothing to you?'

'Of course it won't. There is nothing between us.' Thankfully that declaration had sounded more convincing.

'Are you quite sure, *cara*?'

His palm spread across her face, the pad of his thumb caressing the line of her lips, and she hated the way her eyes closed and the sound of her breath was ragged and uneven before a soft sigh slipped from her.

Why should she fight it? Whatever it was that had exploded between them in London was still there. She wanted to experience it again, to lose herself in the moment of oblivion. She wanted him—and didn't having what you shouldn't want get things out of your system?

Dante braced his arm against the wall as he looked down at Piper. His thumb tingled from sliding it over the lips he ached to kiss. He hadn't slept with a woman since that night in London, telling himself he was too busy, but now he knew it was because he'd still wanted Piper. Somehow she'd crossed over the usually impenetrable barriers around his emotions and now, after spending a week with her, he had to accept the truth. He still yearned for her and there was only one way to deal with such needs. Sate them.

He looked down at her. Expectancy was in those luscious green eyes. She wanted him as much as he wanted her. The hot, sultry passion which swirled in her eyes matched that which spiralled deep within him. Pure carnal lust. Just as it had been the night they'd come together so explosively in London. A night which had changed his life in more ways than he'd anticipated since she'd dropped her bombshell news that morning in his office.

'You are so beautiful.' His thoughts became words—not out of a need to charm, as was his usual seduction routine, but because he wanted her to know what he truly felt. 'And all I want to do right now is kiss you.'

She wrapped her arms around his neck and he pushed his body against her, pinning her to the wall, delving his fingers in the mass of soft red curls which framed her face. His eyes met hers briefly as their faces almost touched, and it satisfied him to see insatiable desire spark higher than ever, setting off a wild reaction within him.

She was his. This woman was his. And tonight he would reclaim her in the most basic way. He lowered his head, intending to brush his lips over hers and tease her into wanting him, but drew in a sharp breath as her lips met his, the need in them undeniable as she took control of the kiss, demanding almost too much from him.

He cursed in Italian against her mouth, tasting her as he did so, tasting her hunger and the desire which matched his, spark for spark. He pressed her harder against the wall, feeling her breasts against his chest and her hips moving wantonly, making him harder than he'd ever been.

He pulled back, briefly stunned by the ferocity of the desire which had leapt like flames around them. The fire of lust threatened to claim them, and right now it was all he wanted.

Piper plunged her fingers into his hair, pulling him back to her. 'Kiss me,' she demanded, and he smiled as he recognised the woman he'd made love to in London.

The hot temptress who'd pushed him further than any woman had ever done was back, and this time she wouldn't be slipping away. Not until he was ready to let her go.

'I intend to do more than kiss you.' The guttural growl which left him sounded positively feral, and his whole body pulsed with desire, demanding immediate satisfaction.

Before he could say anything else she pressed her lips against his once more, the kiss demanding and erotic. She gasped into his mouth as his tongue met hers, sending his heart rate soaring. Only once before had he experienced such wild passion, such fierce desire, and that had been with this woman. The one who'd given her virginity to him and now carried his child. She was truly his. No matter what happened that would never change.

He slid his palm down her throat, pausing as her kiss deepened, became more demanding. Then he moved his hand over her breast, her nipple a tight bud beneath the fabric of her dress, and he had an uncontrollable urge to rip the fabric from her, to expose the delicious breasts so he could taste them and nip at them with his teeth until she cried out with pleasure as she had done that last time.

'Dante...' She groaned his name softly against his lips and pressed her hips tighter against him.

An explosion of hot need was rushing through him.

There wouldn't be any stopping now. This fiery desire had to meet its conclusion, and fast.

While he kissed her, teasing her tongue with his, he slid his hand down to her waist then on to her hips, grasping the fabric of the dress and rucking it up until he could move his hand inside it and feel the soft, warm skin of her thigh. She stopped kissing him and he looked at her as desire throbbed relentlessly in every part of him, demanding satisfaction.

The look in those green eyes still dared him, still goaded him to take her. Her breath was fast and hard, her lips bruised, but still it wasn't enough. He began to stroke her gently with his fingers, and watched as she held her breath when he touched her through her panties. She was as hot for him as he was for her.

'Do you still dare me?' he said hoarsely as he ceased his exploration, moving instead back to her hips and the thin strip of lace which was all that stopped him from claiming her as his once more.

Anger sparked in her eyes, making fireworks of passion and fury explode in them.

'Yes,' she whispered raggedly as her fingers entwined in the hair at the nape of his neck, sending shivers of pleasure he'd never known before down his back. 'I still dare you.'

He held her gaze as he hitched his fingers around the lace and gently pulled. She continued to glare at him, and that mix of anger and fiery passion was almost his undoing. She raised her brow, its slender arch lifting higher in the most alluring way.

'Are you sure, *cara*?'

'I dare you,' she whispered fiercely, in a sexy and husky way, doing untold things to him.

In one swift tug he'd pulled her tiny lace panties apart at the seam.

'Dante!' She gasped in surprise, but made no move to prevent anything else he might do.

'And do you still insist there is nothing between us?'

'Yes.' Her green eyes widened as he moved his hand, trailing his fingers through the curls which shielded her hot, feminine warmth. 'Nothing at all.'

'Yet you want my touch, don't you, *cara*?'

She closed her eyes as he slid his fingers between her thighs. Hot need pulsed through him as he felt how much she wanted him, but he *had* to remain in control. He had to be the one to lead this frenzied and unexpected dance of desire.

'Dante, we can't… Please don't…' She gasped as his touch teased her, pushing her closer and closer to the brink.

'We can and we will.'

He continued to touch and explore her, increasing his need to thrust deep into her—but first he wanted to push her to a climax, to prove how much she wanted him. She writhed against him and clung to him as that climax shook over her body. She was so responsive, so hot. He wanted her right there, against the wall. He couldn't stop now.

Piper opened her eyes, hardly able to believe what had just happened. She felt weak, but still wanted more, and that heady need drove any last remnants of sense from her mind as her shaking hands moved downward to unfasten his trousers. She had to feel him. She had to touch him in the same mind-blowing way he'd touched her. And more importantly she had to take back the control he'd stolen from her with such alarming ease.

He bowed his head almost to her shoulder as with one hand he intervened and freed the hard length of his erection. She felt its heated hardness as he nipped at her neck, the sensation so wild, so new and exciting, she thought she might lose her mind. A deep growl came from him as she wrapped her fingers around him.

Before she could act on any of the new and strange needs filling her body Dante lifted her up. Instinctively she wrapped her legs around him, using the wall behind her to keep her where she wanted to be—intimately against him.

He looked at her, his eyes so black with desire, so intense, they sent a shower of need all over her. Emboldened by the power she now seemed to possess over him, she moved her hips until she could feel the heat of him touch her.

Something wild and unknown was whipping around them like a storm, and it spiralled ever higher. All she could do was look down into the blackness of his eyes as he held her and then the storm stilled. The air around them was heavy with expectancy. She'd heard of the eye of the storm, but had never expected it be like this— with a man like Dante Mancini.

'Dante?' she said expectantly, wanting more and yet suddenly wondering if she'd gone too far.

His answer was a demanding and bruising kiss, and she closed her eyes as his tongue forced itself into her mouth, starting up the wild and erotic dance once more. She moved her hips as he held her against the wall, positioning herself so that she could feel him, tease him, punish him.

A fluid Italian curse left his lips as he broke the kiss to pull back slightly and look at her. Again that expectancy filled the air. His eyes turned sinfully black and he moved with her. In that moment she realised she hadn't been in control at all—she hadn't even been the one teasing or punishing him. But she didn't care about any of that any more. All she wanted was Dante deep inside her. *Now.*

As if he'd read her thoughts he thrust into her, pushing her hard against the wall as his fingers gripped her naked thighs, keeping her just where he wanted her. Just where she wanted to be. She clung to him as if her life depended on it. Maybe it did.

Passion engulfed her as he pulled back, then thrust into her again. An explosion of pulsing need erupted inside her as each thrust took him deeper into her. She moved with him, as if her body had been born to do this with him. He'd awoken the woman in her that night in London, and now all she wanted was to be totally possessed by him.

As she moved his lips sought hers in a kiss so wild and passionate her head spun with dizziness and she closed her eyes, giving herself up to the sensation of being Dante's. With each passing second their breaths became harder and faster. Erratically he kissed down her throat as she let her head fall back against the wall, unable to do anything other than follow the moment.

'Dante!' she cried out as he pushed her higher and faster towards yet another climax. Each frenzied move he made was taking him deeper inside her, exactly where she wanted him to be.

His reply, savage and foreign, only heightened her need for him and she moved with him in a wild dance where all sense or reason was lost.

'You are mine, Piper—*mine.*'

As the world around her exploded his hoarsely whispered words didn't mean anything and she cried out again, aware of Dante's harsh cries as he too found his release.

She clung to him as her body began to shake but didn't dare say anything. Her pulse slowed and she knew she'd played a dangerous game—and lost. The last words he'd said before they'd both exploded with desire had been triumphant, proving that whatever had sparked between them in London was still there and that she wanted him as much as ever.

He looked at her, his dark eyes still wild and full of desire. Slowly he released her, and when her feet touched the floor she was glad of the wall for support. Without a word he took her hand and led her to the stairs.

This wasn't finished yet—and neither did she want it to be.

CHAPTER EIGHT

PIPER LAY CONTENTED in Dante's arms, her back pressed against him as he held her. She studied the gold signet ring on his right hand as he slept. The elaborate 'A' clearly meant something. Was it the initial of a woman who had broken his heart, making it impossible for him to love again? Was that why he was always so cold and calculated?

Dante stirred and she turned round in his embrace to look at him. With his hair tousled from lovemaking and then sleep he looked irresistible, but she would have to resist him. Now was not the time to risk falling for him and she suspected she was perilously close to doing just that. Right now there were practical issues to discuss.

'*Buongiorno, mia cara.*'

His husky voice was as sexy as he looked, and she wondered if she hadn't left him in that hotel in London whether she would have woken to such a warm greeting. Would he have been as pleased to see her in his bed as he was now? Probably not. She wouldn't have had anything to offer him then—nothing to barter with as she did now. No, she was right to have left that night. But she was glad she knew what it was like to wake within the warm embrace of this man's arms.

'Morning.' Shyness crept over her.

'You didn't run out on me this time, *cara*.'

His eyes darkened, and she knew she would have to leave the bed before he convinced her otherwise.

'No, but that's exactly what I am about to do now.' She threw back the covers and tried hard to pretend that she didn't care at all that she was naked and that he was watching her every move.

'And why would that be?'

A shiver of pleasure slithered down her spine. His voice was tantalisingly sexy but she ignored it and grabbed her robe and headed for the shower.

'We have things to discuss about our deal and where we go from here.'

She spoke over her shoulder, and without waiting for his response went into the en-suite shower room and turned on the shower, trying not to think too hard about the fact that their engagement would not only help him get the deal he wanted so badly, and salvage his reputation with the charity, it would also involve their families. Neither of them had a father in their lives, but their mothers deserved to know about the baby, be a part of its life.

She discarded her robe and stepped under the warm jets, closing her eyes as the water cascaded over her. She could still hear her mother's voice when they'd spoken after her arrival in Rome. It had only been then that she'd been brave enough to tell her about Dante, knowing that it might very easily appear in the press, and she still needed to tell her about the baby.

Lost in thought, she didn't hear Dante as he stepped into the shower, and she gave a startled cry as he pulled her against him. Through the warmth of the water pounding down on her she was in no doubt of his intentions.

'What are you doing?' She laughed, never having expected this. It was something lovers would do, wasn't it? And she and Dante were as far from being lovers as they had ever been.

'Making the most of this gorgeous body whilst it's still naked.' He kissed her—a long, lingering kiss—and her senses became heightened by the water as it spilled over them and she willingly kissed him back, wanting this last moment of passion with him before she broached the subject of their engagement and what it would mean to everyone.

'Come back to bed,' he said in a husky voice.

The fire of desire was burning bright in his eyes, fuelling her own even more. He turned off the shower and took her hand and led her out, pausing to wrap her in a large towel. She cuddled into it, sneaking a glance at him as he took a smaller towel and dried his body before wrapping it around his hips. That didn't quell the throb of desire just being this close to him ignited, and the slow burn of desire rose inside her once more.

Before she could say anything he led her back to the bedroom, back to the large bed and the rumpled cream sheets, tossing aside the distinctly masculine bronze covers.

'I intend to make love to you again before we discuss anything.'

'But we should talk.'

'No talking.'

He pushed her gently back onto the bed, the towel she clutched around her falling open, exposing her to his gaze. But he didn't take advantage of that for too long. He dropped the towel he'd slung around his hips to the floor and joined her on the bed, kissing down her body. As he reached her still flat stomach he pressed light feathery kisses to it, and in her lust-drugged stupor she imagined him kissing his child. His hands caressed her waist in the most loving of gestures and she had to squeeze her eyes shut against a tear that threatened to fall.

Piper clutched at the sheets when he moved lower, hardly able to believe the sensations rushing around her. Love and lust were becoming entwined and she knew it was dangerous. This wouldn't sort things out, but it was certainly a distraction she was prepared to endure. He made her feel alive. He made her feel beautiful. And after years of thinking she didn't deserve love it was almost too much—because this wasn't love. It could never be love.

He kissed his way back up, over her stomach to her breasts, teasing each hardened nipple in turn before moving over her, the hardness of his erection encouraging her to become his once more. It was a temptation too much and she welcomed him into her, relished the fizz of desire with each move he made and abandoned herself to the moment once more.

Dante's body still hummed from the amazing sex he'd enjoyed with Piper since they'd returned to his villa last night. He'd never intended to take her so roughly, and especially not against the wall in his living room, but she did something to him no other woman had done. Just as she had done that night in his hotel room in London. She made him lose control, made him forget everything. She drove him wild.

Now he watched her cross the living room to join him as he sat in front of a newly lit fire. It might not be winter yet but he wanted the comfort of it and the way it made him relax, and he wanted to share this special time with Piper. For the first time ever he wanted to allow a woman close—for a while at least.

'Oh, an open fire. Now, *that's* something I'm not used to.' She smiled at him and sat in a large chair, curling her jean-clad legs under her.

'It's much better from over here.' He surprised himself by inviting her to come closer to him. It might be down to the way he always felt relaxed here, or the intimacy they'd shared since arriving, but he wanted her close. He'd never wanted *anyone* close. What was happening to him?

'I guess so.' Shyness entered her voice and a blush spread over her cheeks as she went to sit on the sofa next to him, concentrating intently on the fire as if she couldn't look at him. 'It's quite romantic, really.'

Romantic? Had he been trying for 'romantic' when he'd lit it, envisaging them curled up together enjoying each other's company? He'd wanted to escape everything, just for today, but romance was the last thing he wanted to make her think of. He didn't believe in romance and definitely didn't want it in his life. Such things led to more complicated emotions like love, and that was something he didn't want to tango with—for any price.

'I find a fire relaxing,' he said guardedly. 'It's one of my winter pleasures when I'm here at the villa.'

'We do need to talk.' She spoke with caution and glanced across at him. 'About last night.'

'Do you mean the amazing success you made of coaxing Bettino D'Antonio round with your talk of art, or what happened when we returned?' He also spoke with caution, anxious that she didn't make too much of the hours they'd spent in bed, the amount of times they'd had sex. He never thought of it as making love. That would give it an entirely different meaning.

'The dinner.' Indignation cracked in her voice. 'Do you really think Bettino was impressed?'

Dante moved across the sofa towards her, took her hand and pressed her fingers to his lips. '*Mia cara*, you positively charmed him, and I am certain that it will be not one but two contracts which will be coming our way.'

He had a good feeling about the deal now, and he knew he had Piper to thank for that. Her talk of art, of wanting to run her own curating business, had been so spontaneous, so full of enthusiasm, D'Antonio had been unable to resist her—and if truth be told neither had he. He'd sat and watched as her eyes had sparkled with genuine joy and shone with pleasure whilst she was talking about art. He'd also been just a little put out that he hadn't known exactly how important the subject was to her. She'd told him she liked to visit art galleries, but it was obvious it was far more than that.

'But I'm not qualified. I didn't finish my course and I don't have a business.' She paled as the implications hit her. 'I can't take a contract—not when there are good companies out there already. And there's the baby...'

'A business can be started right now if you want. Your knowledge of the subject is more than enough.'

'You don't know that.'

'I'm sure it's sufficient, at least. How far into your degree were you?'

'I'd nearly finished. I was in my last year when my father got sick. I only had my final exams to do, really. I meant to go back, but...'

'That's more than enough to start with. And a commission from D'Antonio would set you up—if that's what you want.'

'I'll think about it.'

The reservation in her voice made him want to hold her and tell her he'd help her. Why did he want to do that? Why did he feel the need to tangle himself up emotionally with this woman more than he already was?

He shrugged, letting her hand go, and sat back, studying her pensive expression. There was more—much more to her reservation. He could feel it.

'I have other things to do first.'

She looked up at him and he held her gaze, challenging her to speak her mind, say what was bothering her—because something was.

'What is so important, Piper?'

She looked uncertainly at him and apprehension settled over him, suffocating the relaxed peace he'd found.

'I'd like us both to go to London.' After holding his gaze for the briefest of moments she looked down, her long lashes shutting him out.

'Is there something in particular you wish to do there? Somewhere you want to be seen to validate our engagement?' He kept his voice light, but inside the fingers of dread were closing in, threatening to choke him. This woman, who'd claimed to want nothing from him, now seemed to want much more than he could ever give.

'Yes.' She nodded. 'I'd like us to see my mother.'

The thump to his chest as the reality of his fears hit him was hard. 'No. This engagement is to secure a business deal and to legitimise our child. There is no need to bring family members into it.'

Unease shrouded him. What would *his* mother think when she read in the papers or the glossy magazines that he was to be married? Worse still, that he was to be a father?

'Surely *your* mother will want to know? Even if you can't tell her the sordid truth.'

The spike of hurt in her voice should have made him feel guilty, but already he could feel his emotions closing off, feel himself withdrawing. They'd shared a night of passion and it should have changed nothing, but somehow it had changed everything.

'My mother will know only what she has to, and I suggest you do the same with your mother. This is not a real engagement and there isn't any need to complicate it further.' Anger surged through him as he fought back the fear of what his mother would think of his latest deal, of the false hope he might give her that he'd finally left the past behind.

'Haven't we already done that with last night?'

She hurled the accusation at him, her green eyes wide and full of hurt. Already he was upsetting her, causing her pain. As soon as he became close to anyone he did something to hurt them or turn them away, until ultimately they left his life.

'*You* complicated things in London, leading me to believe protection wasn't required.' Immediately he took his usual stance of self-defence, angry that she'd made him feel and, worse, that he cared how *she* felt.

'No wonder your brother left home as soon as he could!'

Dante saw a mist of red descend at the mention of Alessio. As if he didn't already have enough to worry about, she'd opened that wound too. '*Never* bring my brother into this. He and my mother are the reason I fought to make a living, the reason I had to make something of myself. Everything I did, I did for them. I wanted to give them a better life, but it was too late for my brother.'

She looked up at him, her earlier prickly demeanour evaporating. 'Too late? Why?'

The questions filled the void which had opened up between them, connecting them once more in a way he wasn't sure he could handle.

'My brother kept the wrong company, and after he became a teenager he was always in trouble.' Dante felt the pull of the connection between him and Piper just as surely as he felt her sympathetic gaze on him. He sensed the danger in opening himself up, exposing emotions he'd buried many years ago.

'What happened?'

She looked as beautiful as he'd ever seen her. But something inside him had changed. She'd opened a door he'd closed and forgotten about. A door that couldn't be closed again now.

Mentally he shook himself. It wouldn't do either of them any good to be weighed down with emotions. 'He resented my authority over him and rebelled against anything I said.'

'But isn't that what all teenagers do?'

Her smile was warm as she leaned closer. He inhaled her perfume, the same scent which had tormented him in the elevator at his office the morning after his meeting with Xander, Zayn and Benjamin. His life was unrecognisable now.

'Not all teenagers run away, leaving behind a distraught mother.' He gritted his teeth together as the sound of his mother's sobs filled his mind. Piper had opened up the memory and now he couldn't stop it coming back.

'Did you find him? I mean…he *did* come back, didn't he?' She stumbled over her words, probably due to the anger that must be clearly etched on his face. Damn it, he had no wish to talk about this with anyone—least of all this woman.

The pain of those first days after Alessio had gone still haunted him. Every time he'd looked at his mother he'd known she blamed *him*, known it was his fault. He'd driven Alessio away. He'd tried to be a father figure before he had really become a man himself, taking on the role of disciplining his wild brother when he had been only seventeen. For three years a battle of wills had raged between him and Alessio—until his sixteenth birthday. The day he'd walked out of the small house where his mother had struggled to bring them up. It had been the last time they'd seen him alive.

'We had no idea where he was for four years.'

'So you *did* find him?'

Dante recalled the horror of the day he'd found out the truth of Alessio's disappearance. The fact that his brother had died alone years before was something he could never forgive himself for.

'I found out that he'd died alone at the age of eighteen.'

The gasp of shock which came from Piper told him what he already knew. It was shocking, and it was *his* fault. He stared into the flames of the fire which had cooled to a gentle orange glow, wrapping around the logs. He couldn't look at Piper. He didn't want to see the shock or the blame on her face. It would only confirm what he'd believed ever since that day.

'That is so sad,' she said in a whisper, but still he couldn't look at her.

'He died at the hands of a rival street gang. It was my fault. I should have made him come home when he first left. It was my job to keep him safe.'

She touched his arm and he looked at her. The compassion in her eyes was too much. 'It's *not* your fault, Dante.'

'I failed him, Piper. I failed him *and* my mother. I didn't do what I was supposed to do. I didn't protect and care for them.'

When Piper had told him she was carrying his child he'd appeared to give more importance to the deal and salvaging his reputation, but it was the need to look after her and his baby which had driven him to such drastic action. He'd never thought it would be possible for him to care, to want to put himself in a vulnerable position again, but as soon as he'd known why she'd come to Rome it had been the only thing he wanted to do.

Piper looked at Dante. The pain in his eyes was too much to bear and she wanted to hold him, tell him it wasn't his fault and try and ease his pain—just as he had done for her when she'd finally confessed to the blindness which had affected her left eye since birth. That hadn't mattered to him and this didn't matter to her. She wanted him to see he *wasn't* to blame—not when he'd been so young himself.

'You mustn't blame yourself,' she said, and gently squeezed his arm, wanting to offer some kind of comfort.

'You don't know anything about it.' He pulled his arm free of her touch, and the rejection stung her far more than any icy words.

'I want to know.' She watched as he pressed his thumb and finger against his signet ring, just as he'd done whilst she'd read over the contract he'd drawn up. He'd stood over her then and tension had crackled in the air, just as it did now. 'What if I meet your mother? Shouldn't I at least know something?'

He swore harshly in Italian, but she resisted the urge to step back and drop the subject. She needed to know about his past. Not only because she might meet someone who knew, but because she wanted to—for her child. His mother was her child's grandmother. Could he deny her that?

'There will be no meeting between you and my mother. I will explain the true situation to her, and I suggest you tell yours. That way neither of us will give false hope to anyone.'

'False hope of what? Love and happiness?' She tried to keep the hurt from sounding in her voice, but his rejection of her cut deep. Even so, what he said made sense. Maybe telling her mother the truth, instead of dressing it up as a fairytale romance, would be best. At least that way she wouldn't have to explain when he walked away from her, leaving her a single mother, alone in the world except for her own mother.

'Love and happiness are for fools,' he said, and scowled at her, reminding her of that morning in his office when she had been positively the last person he'd wanted to find waiting for him. He touched his ring again, drawing her attention back to his brother.

'Whatever happened to your brother, it's *not* your fault.' She moved towards him again, desperate to know more and understand.

'I wanted to make a better life for my mother. She had a tough time bringing up two boys alone and in poverty, and Alessio was wilful and rebellious even as a child.'

Piper recalled the article she'd read in *Celebrity Spy!* Whilst going to great lengths to expose his playboy lifestyle, it had credited him with having made his own fortune. Had he really been motivated by the need to provide for his brother Alessio?

She looked at him, then at his hand. 'Was the ring his?'

The question was out before she could think, before she could stop it, and for a second the air around her froze as he looked at her. She bit her bottom lip and watched as he looked down at his right hand, at the gold signet ring she'd studied as he'd slept beside her that morning.

'I bought it for his sixteenth birthday and planned to give it to him that evening, after a family meal, but Alessio had other ideas and he'd long since gone. I spent the night consoling my mother and being angry with him, wanting only to banish the selfish youngster from my mind and my life.'

She put her hand to her mouth to stifle a gasp of shock, but it still slipped out. 'That must have been terrible for your mother.'

'I have never forgiven myself for doing that to her.'

'You?'

'If I hadn't ruled Alessio so hard, trying to shape him into the man I wanted him to be instead of allowing him to find out who he was, this conversation wouldn't be happening.'

'I still don't see how it's your fault,' she said, exasperation getting the better of her.

'That, *cara*, is because you do not know me. Nothing good will come of you being entangled in my life.'

'Our child will come of it, and to me that is good.' She flung the words at him, angry that he wouldn't let her close, wouldn't let her past the invisible barrier he had around him.

Slowly he moved towards her and reached out, touching her face. Her anger melted away and she yearned for more than a caress to her face.

'You have a very generous nature. Never let anyone change that. Least of all me.'

Before she could say anything else he brushed his lips over hers and her eyelashes fluttered down. As he moved back, away from her, it was as if he was going behind a barrier of ice. She could still see him, but the coldness in his eyes, the frozen set of his shoulders, warned her that what they'd shared during the weekend was finished.

'What happened between us here is over. We made our deal and stated our terms and now it is time to bring it all to a conclusion.'

CHAPTER NINE

THEIR FIRST MORNING back in Rome, Piper awoke alone in the bed—just as Dante had warned her. After an exquisite weekend entwined around his lean body she knew that what they'd shared in Tuscany was over. He had a deal to secure and she had a role to play.

She'd sensed his withdrawal as he'd driven them back to Rome. Each passing hour had distanced him from the man he'd been in Tuscany. He'd returned to being the man she'd seen arriving at his office that morning, the aloof man who trusted nobody and kept everyone at a distance. The ruthless businessman was back.

She slipped from the bed, her limbs still aching from the hours of wonderful sex with Dante. How could she, an innocent woman who'd had no experience of men before she'd met Dante, have become such a different woman? One who matched his expertise and skill as a lover? Without even touching her he'd had her yearning for him. And she'd responded with eagerness, wanting to give him as much pleasure as he gave her.

Even though her body belonged to him she couldn't give him her heart, couldn't allow herself to fall for him. Whatever it was between them, it had to stay as lust—although if she was brave enough to admit it she'd acknowledge that her emotions had long since passed that point. Something she had to conceal from him. The deal they'd struck was just that. A deal.

She pushed back a wave of nausea and strengthened her resolve to put aside her emotions as she made her way to the doors leading onto the terrace. She'd quickly realised he favoured the outdoors in the mornings, even though winter had brought a chill to the air.

'Good morning,' she said.

'I had not expected you to be up yet.'

He strode over from where he'd been standing, looking out over the city, moving back inside, and as he passed she caught his freshly showered scent and aftershave. He poured coffee and she tried hard to regain her assaulted senses from the strong aroma. For a moment, as dizziness and nausea took charge and she clung to the doorframe, she wasn't aware that he was talking to her.

'Are you well?'

'I…' Her head spun and words refused to form. She reached for the back of a chair in a desperate attempt to remain standing as her stomach turned over and blackness threatened to claim her.

She heard Dante's angry words as she closed her eyes. She wanted to fight it, but couldn't, and she let herself slip into the calm oblivion of darkness. Then she felt his arms around her, her body pressed against the safety and strength of his, and forced her eyes open, forced her head to stop spinning.

He looked down at her as he lifted her into his arms. 'You are going back to bed to wait for the doctor.'

She wanted to fight him, wanted to tell him that most women felt faint and suffered sickness in pregnancy, but she was scared. She'd never felt so ill in her life, so weak and defeated. Surely this wasn't right? But she had nobody to ask for reassurance—nobody but Dante. She was completely at his mercy.

She closed her eyes as another wave of dizziness hurtled over her.

'The fact that you are unable to argue with me is worrying,' he said, and she opened her eyes again, allowing the deep tones of his voice to drag her back from the dark oblivion her body so desperately sought.

She fought the hurt which spiked through her at the angry tone of his words. Where was the tender and gentle man she'd made love with yesterday morning as the sun had risen over the Tuscan hills? What had happened to the man who'd opened up to her, pulling down his barriers to let her into his world?

He'd shared things with her she suspected he hadn't shared for a long time. If he'd kept those barriers lowered for long enough would she have found a warm and loving man who was hurting and blaming himself for something which wasn't his fault? A man who needed love? Could she love the man she'd seen that day in Tuscany?

Yes, she could.

The realisation hit her as his hold on her tightened, but she couldn't allow herself to love this man. He looked down at her, fierce hardness etched on his handsome face as he negotiated the furniture and took her back to the bedroom she'd just left.

He laid her on the bed, his arms lingering around her, keeping her close and reminding her of the passion they'd shared over the weekend. Her gaze met his and the caramel-brown of his eyes darkened, the emotion within them unreadable. She drew in a breath which sounded as ragged as if he'd just kissed her and he pulled himself away, pressing his palm briefly against her forehead before standing tall at the bedside. For a moment she thought she saw genuine concern in his eyes, but quickly it was chased away by hard anger.

'I wanted to talk about our need to do more to create a love affair real enough to silence the gossips of the world, But not now. You need to rest.'

A tremor of sickness and disappointment washed over Piper. The only thing he was concerned about was his stupid deal. 'Very well,' she said as he looked down at her, feeling the warmth of his touch still on her forehead. 'Our charade will continue until there isn't a shred of doubt that you are a reformed man.'

She couldn't keep the spike of anger from her voice as panic rushed over her. What if he backed out of the deal now? What if he refused to have anything to do with their child?

'Not until you are well. Think of the baby, Piper, and do as I say. Just for once.' Exasperation entwined with anger, making each word short and sharp.

So he cared about the baby, did he? Suddenly she felt very scared—for herself and for the baby. She turned away from him as tears began to slip down her cheeks. This wasn't what she'd come to Rome for. A fake engagement to further his business was not worth risking her baby over, and that was what she was doing now. Risking her baby.

Tears cascaded down her face, but she kept her face hidden from him, not wanting to see the anger in those eyes or the harsh lines of annoyance on his face. Finally she heard him leave, and his fluid Italian curse could not be mistaken as his footsteps receded.

Guilt hung over Dante as he waited for the doctor to come out of Piper's room. He'd done it again. Let down someone who was relying on him. He hadn't cared for Piper as he should have, had thought of nothing but himself, and now she was ill. Worse than that, his selfish need to get the deal of a lifetime had put his baby at risk.

He closed his eyes against such dark thoughts, against the past mingling menacingly with the present. What if she lost the baby—*his* baby? It would be his fault. Just as Alessio leaving home had been.

With alarming clarity he realised he wanted this child, his son or daughter, but that didn't alter the fact that the woman who carried his child had agreed to his suggested deal, creating her own terms. Neither did it change the fact that after the way he'd handled things with Alessio he wasn't fit to be a father.

The click of the door as the doctor came out jolted him from that dark and painful thought. He wanted to ask if she was going to be okay, if the baby was well, but his mouth had become dry and words refused to form.

'Your fiancée and your baby need rest, Signor Mancini, and love and care.' The old man's smile was in total contrast to the warning tone of his voice. Or was that guilt, making him imagine the doctor's disapproval?

'Then rest is what she will have,' he said, firmly putting aside the option of love and care. He couldn't do either. Piper would be better without him in her life, but what of his child—his flesh and blood? Could he allow the past to chase him away from his own child? Even if it was a child he'd never intended to have… never wanted?

'I will call again tomorrow.'

'*Grazie.*'

He couldn't say anything else and for a moment stood looking at the door of the bedroom, terrified of the future that lay within. Already he'd hurt Piper, pushed her too hard in creating their fake love affair, insisting on changing her and parading her around Rome. Once they'd arrived in Tuscany their time at the villa had been so different, so unexpected. He'd gone back on his self-made promise and had lost control. As if he'd wanted to see what he could have if only he opened himself up to feeling emotion. Had *he* caused this? Had his selfish desire for her made her ill?

He walked slowly into the bedroom, the accusations of the past walking alongside him like dark shadows. He wanted to protect and care for Piper, but how could he when his heart was stone-cold? How could he when he'd already proved he wasn't fit to be a father?

'I'm sorry to be a nuisance,' she said as she propped herself up against the pillows, tears still shining in her eyes. Tears *he* was responsible for.

Something clutched at his heart, squeezing it hard, but all he could feel was guilt. 'It is me who should apologise,' he said crisply, averting his gaze from her still pale face to look out through the window over the rooftops of Rome. 'I expected too much.'

'But what about the party this evening? How can we convince everyone if I am not with you?'

A tremor of panic wobbled in her voice, ratcheting up his guilt.

'There will be other parties. You must rest for the baby's sake.' He turned to look at her and the worried frown on her face cut deep into his heart, proving he wasn't as cold and detached as he'd thought.

'I just want all this over, Dante.'

She swallowed hard and took a deep breath, and he looked into her eyes, where beneath the tiredness he saw fierce determination.

'There is nothing we can do about the deal but wait.'

Compelled to go to her, he sat down on the edge of the bed and took her hand in his. What was it about this woman that made rational and sensible thought almost impossible? She'd changed him, made him yearn for things that were impossible. Was it that hint of what might have been if his past hadn't blocked the way what made her so alluring, so very tempting and irresistible?

'Is that all that's important to you, Dante? The deal?'

Piper couldn't keep the disappointment from her voice. After everything they'd shared at the weekend, all the barriers which had been broken down, he still only wanted the deal.

She held her breath as Dante moved back towards the bed and sat down on the edge, taking her hand in his. She looked at her pale skin against his tanned hands and as his fingers tightened around hers couldn't ignore how safe it made her feel. His hand was warm and large and very comforting.

'All I want is for you to get well.'

Dante's voice, soft and alarmingly sexy, drew her gaze up and to his face. Something new and unreadable was in his eyes, making her breath catch audibly in her throat.

'You wouldn't have become ill if things had been different, had gone as planned.'

Piper watched as his free hand closed over the top of hers, making pulling her hand away impossible—just as pulling back her emotions was becoming so difficult. The only thing which hadn't gone according to the terms of the deal they'd agreed was their time in Tuscany. Their weekend of being lovers. Did he regret it?

'What things?' she asked, needing to know what was going on. She was falling deeper and harder for him and she had to know how he felt. He was such a closed-off man, this might be her only chance.

'We agreed that not being intimate was part of the deal. "A marriage on paper" was, I think, the term you used.'

His fingers were caressing her hand, distracting her from thinking too deeply about what she'd said and what she'd allowed to happen. She was about to tell him that when he spoke again.

'I should have had more control.'

'Dante, you mustn't blame yourself all the time.' Her voice was a whisper as he looked directly into her eyes as if searching for the truth. For a brief moment she thought he might lean forward and kiss her. Instead he spoke firmly, and the moment of reflection was over.

'We are both responsible for what happened in Tuscany.'

How could she tell him she'd been so desperate for his touch, his kiss, that she would have sold her soul to the devil if it had meant she could be his once more? What would he think of her if she did?

'It won't happen again. You have my word.'

He withdrew his hands, leaving hers feeling cold. She pulled away, clutching both hands against her to deflect the pain those words had caused. She didn't want his word. She wanted it to happen again. She wanted to be loved by him. Truly loved.

'Then we still have a deal.' The words shot from her before she had time to consider their meaning.

He stood up, a hardened glint in his eyes, the softness of moments ago gone. '*Va bene*. As soon as you are rested we shall resume our act of lovers. There are many more events in coming days where our appearance together will set the tongues of gossip wagging.'

Inside, the weakness which had washed over her that morning slipped away and a steely determination to finish this once and for all replaced it. Reassured by the doctor that she'd just been doing too much, and the baby wasn't in any danger, she was now determined to achieve her part of the deal. All she had to keep telling herself was that this was for her baby, to keep its father in their lives.

'As I said, I just want to get this over with. So please make whatever arrangements you want for tomorrow night.' Her voice was hard, but it didn't appear to affect him at all.

'There is an opera tomorrow night I'd like us to attend. If the doctor assures me everything is as it should be we shall attend.' Any hint of concern had left his face and his voice. The mercenary man who'd put the deal to her was back—and firmly in control.

'Everything is fine, Dante. It is normal for a woman to feel unwell early in her pregnancy.' She tried to keep her voice light, but couldn't look at him.

'That may be so, but I will not take any risks.'

Piper's heart thumped ever harder. Was he trying to say he cared about her—or more? Did this mean what they'd shared in Tuscany had been real and not just a moment of lust?

Before she could say anything, or allow those thoughts to grow, his firm words cut down any hope. 'The baby is vital to this deal.'

With those cruel words lingering in the air, he left, unaware of just how much emotional pain she was in after stupidly believing there was the hope of something more between them—something they could build on for their child's future happiness.

CHAPTER TEN

THE FOLLOWING EVENING Dante waited on the terrace as the lights of Rome sparkled around him. He felt free out here, free to think—or at least that was how it had been until he'd let Piper into his life. Now she filled his every thought, sneaking in where no woman had ever been, making everything complicated. On top of that, his mother had heard of their engagement and despite his denial that he'd fallen in love, despite his telling her that it was purely for business, she was pushing to meet his fiancée. Guilt had sliced into him at the obvious hope in her voice that it was really something more.

'I wasn't sure what an evening at the opera required.'

Piper's now familiar accent cut him off from his thoughts and he turned to see her standing in front of the open doors which led back into his apartment. The light from within filtered around her, showcasing her curves and making him want things he had no right to want. He'd never seen her look so beautiful—or desirable. The red dress she wore was moulded to her body, and the way the fabric crossed over her breasts to form straps caught his attention, infusing him with the kind of need he'd been valiantly denying since their time in Tuscany.

'Red is perfect,' he snapped ungraciously as he

fought down memories of their time together over the weekend—time that could not be repeated.

He'd thought that by giving in to the lust he'd still had for her since London the desire would go. That was all it usually took for his interest in a woman to wane. But then he'd never met a woman like Piper—a woman who made him feel different, made him long for things the likes of which he had no right to want. Not when he'd messed up his brother's and his mother's life. The reality of it was that he wasn't any better than his father, and that was something he'd promised himself as a young man that he would be.

'In that case I'm ready to leave.'

She clutched a silver purse and as she turned, lifting the skirt of her dress to step back into the apartment, he noticed silver sandals, the straps around her ankles suddenly the sexiest thing he'd ever seen.

Did they *have* to go out this evening? The thought of staying in filled his mind, stoking the embers of passion which had burned bright in Tuscany. The thought of relaxing in Piper's company before taking her to bed—*his* bed, not the damned spare room.

He cursed under his breath. No. The charade of their engagement had to be played out. He had to remember why he'd even agreed to it in the first place.

Benjamin Carter's words came unbidden from the back of his mind where he'd relegated them. *'We need to find women who are happy to marry quickly and conveniently. Women we can trust, who will be discreet. Loyal.'*

Piper turned as he entered the apartment. 'Sorry, did you say something?'

'It's time we left. The idea of going to the opera is not

for enjoyment but to make our engagement known— alert the press and offset that article.'

'Yes, I'm aware of that.' Her green eyes speared him with their sudden frostiness.

'Va bene.' He opened the door to his apartment and waited for her to walk through. 'If we get noticed this evening only one or two more dates will be needed, and then hopefully the deal with D'Antonio will be concluded in my favour.'

'Then let's give everyone something to talk about.'

She flounced out and stood in stony silence as the elevator took them down to his waiting car. The silence settled between them as they sat in the back of his car for the short drive to the opera house.

As they entered the grand building he was pleased to see Piper taking her role in his life seriously. She smiled, posing for photographs with him as if she'd been born to a life of high celebrity. She wore the designer clothes with effortless ease, and was so far removed from the redhead who'd sat in his office wearing jeans and a jumper it was unbelievable that it had been little over a week ago.

Even after they'd entered the building and the press had moved their attention to other rich and famous faces Piper kept up the show. He watched her as she spoke with an older couple and knew he should be pleased she'd settled into this new role, but he found it unsettling just how easily she had. She'd moved from being an ordinary girl to one with wealth at her disposal. Playing the role of his fiancée was one she enjoyed, and she seemed determined to sample as much of the lifestyle as she could.

As Piper returned to his side, a genuine smile on her lips, he saw Capricia Conetta bearing down on them and winced inwardly. This would be a true test of Piper's new confident self. Capricia was *not* a woman to hide behind pleasantries.

'*Ciao*, Dante.' The tall, willowy brunette embraced him, kissing him on both cheeks before turning her attention to Piper. 'And *you* are the woman who has managed to persuade the notorious Dante Mancini to put a ring on her finger. Bravo, you. You are obviously a better woman than I am.'

'It was more a case of him persuading *me* to wear it.'

The haughty reply Piper flung at her unknown adversary was unexpected, and Dante resisted the urge to laugh at Capricia's expression.

'Just don't assume you can ever tame him. He is a ruthless man—in the boardroom as well as in the bedroom.' With those spite-laden words hanging in the air, Capricia turned and waltzed off with great drama.

'An ex-lover, by any chance?' Piper turned her attention to him and he nodded, not at all proud to have been associated with such a woman, but before he could respond she quickly added, 'Can we take our seats yet?'

He sensed that the bravado she was hiding behind was in danger of slipping. She wasn't as unaffected by her confrontation with Capricia as she wanted him to think, and she'd gone pale. 'Are you sure you're well enough to go?'

'Of course. The show must go on and all that.'

The bitter snap in her voice told him otherwise, but he guided her to their seats.

'A box?' she queried, a hint of nerves in her voice.

'We are here to be seen. A lovers' date.'

'Of course—how silly of me.'

* * *

For most of the performance Dante had sat on her left and watched Piper, who had been enthralled by all that had happened on the stage. She'd seemed totally oblivious to his presence. He knew it was because he'd been on her blind side, but the fact that she could dismiss him so easily from her mind when he could barely stop thinking about *her* irritated him more than he cared to admit. Not once had she turned to him, shown any display of affection that would have proved to the watching people that they were in love.

Now he sat round a table with four other guests, all of whom were trying to draw as much information as possible from Piper about their engagement. She smiled politely at them, but whenever *he* looked at her she glanced away shyly. The blush that crept over her face should have irritated him, but for some strange reason it didn't. It highlighted how different Piper was from the likes of Capricia, and served only to intensify what he was feeling for her. Even though he wanted to feel nothing at all—for anyone.

'I never thought you'd succumb to marriage,' one man said, and raised his glass at him, irritating Dante further.

But he raised his glass in acknowledgement and recalled his recent conversation with his mother, and her assumption that finally he'd made peace with himself and could settle down and raise a family. If only she knew the truth… But she never would.

'Have you set a date?' an older woman asked Piper, who now turned her attention to him, a smile fixed on her pretty face. But he recognised the message asking for help in her eyes.

'Next summer,' he supplied, and didn't miss the rise of Piper's brows. 'In Tuscany.'

Piper's stomach flipped over at the thought of where she'd be next summer—not only a new mother, but married to the father of her child. How had everything happened so fast when all she'd wanted to do was tell Dante he was to be a father? She'd thought fate had given her a helping hand after she'd seen the article, allowing her to discover the name of the man whose child she carried.

'A summer wedding! You will, of course, have a feature in a magazine?' demanded the woman, before turning her attention to Dante. 'Just make sure it's better than the last one you were named in.'

Piper glanced quickly at Dante, saw his jaw clench against the less than veiled sarcasm and couldn't help herself from reaching out and touching his hand, which was held in a tight fist on the table. He looked abruptly at her and she smiled.

'It will naturally be very different. It will be about what I am certain will be the happiest day of my life.'

Piper's breath caught audibly as he looked at her. The undisguised passion burning in his eyes would leave the older couple in no doubt that he was in love with her. Then, to her surprise, he lifted her fingertips to his lips and kissed them, his gaze firmly fixed on hers.

'Of that I have no doubt,' the older woman said, before launching into an avid discussion in Italian with her husband. And, even though she didn't understand a word, Piper could tell that *she* was the topic of that conversation.

The remainder of the evening went well and Dante's attention to her never once slipped. He'd played his part to perfection, and she too had done the same. She knew he was hoping their engagement would become the talk of Rome society, and that photos of them at the opera would grace the pages of the very magazine which had instigated this whole deal.

All night Piper had tried so hard to keep the smile on her face, but now she ached from the effort and was pleased to be able to shut the door on Rome and the people she'd been mixing with all night. Her nausea hadn't completely abated, and the effort of being an adoring fiancée had become too much. She was exhausted.

She couldn't believe the lifestyle she was now living. It wasn't only the luxury of nice clothes, fabulous places to go or staff on hand to cater to her every need that left her cold—it was the veiled and icy superiority of the people who lived such a life. Whilst Dante appeared comfortable in that world she wasn't entirely convinced he belonged there, or that he wanted to be a part of it. He had seemed more relaxed and happy in Tuscany.

'I'm not sure I enjoy all this attention,' she said as she watched him pour himself a drink.

She should just go straight to bed, but she wouldn't sleep—she was sure of that. Since they'd left the restaurant he'd cooled towards her. His display of affection had been entirely that.

'It takes time to get used to it,' he replied as he put the top back on a crystal decanter, unwittingly giving an answer to her unspoken question.

'How long did it take *you*?'

She wanted to talk, wanted to feel closer to him, to know more of him. Just being physically close wasn't enough—not for her, the girl who'd always dreamt of being whisked away to a happy-ever-after by a knight in shining armour. And even though he was far from that he'd made her feel like a princess this evening.

'I don't recall.' He skilfully evaded her question. 'You look tired. Should you rest? For the sake of the baby?'

So he was concerned—not about her, but the baby. The child he didn't really want…the one that came as part of the deal he'd struck with her to salvage his reputation. Didn't that make him as shallow as all the men and women she'd mixed with tonight?

'Yes, I am.' A hint of concern crossed his handsome face as she spoke a little too sharply. 'I will say good-night.'

'I will be leaving early tomorrow morning,' he said, and took a sip of his brandy, preferring to look at the amber liquid as he swirled it around the glass and not at her. 'But I suggest you have a restful day. We have a party tomorrow evening.'

'What time do you want me ready to perform my duty as your fiancée?' She surprised herself with the fierceness of her question, and if the rise of his brows was anything to go by he too was shocked.

'We shall leave at seven.'

'Very well,' she said as she walked towards the room that should be his. Despite their time in Tuscany, and the passion which had leapt to life, he showed no intention of sharing it with her. She should be glad—it was, after all, what she'd wanted—but the sting of his rejection of her as a woman cut far deeper than she'd thought possible.

She would have to toughen up, otherwise she would never see this wretched deal through. All she needed to do was remember why she was doing it—for her baby.

CHAPTER ELEVEN

PIPER'S ENERGY AND enthusiasm for her role of Dante Mancini's fiancée had all but gone. Dante had become more distant each evening—at least in private. Publically he'd become ever more charming and attentive, which only highlighted his withdrawal.

She glanced out of the window as the car moved through the busy traffic of Rome, trying to quell the now ever-present nausea. At Dante's insistence his doctor had called again today, but had reassured them that it was all part of pregnancy and would pass.

Dante's voice dragged her from her thoughts. 'We will be arriving in just a few minutes. This party is one of the highlights of Rome's social scene and the press will be in full attendance.'

'I understand,' she said, and looked across the car, lit by the lights of Rome. 'Tonight will be no different to the other nights. I intend to keep my side of our deal.'

'Just as I will keep mine.' He looked at her, and for a moment the car zinged with the attraction that still drew her to him.

Did he really mean that?

'I hope so, Dante. *You* are doing this for a deal, but I'm doing it for our child.'

'Also a deal.' The clipped reply not only dried the

conversation, but confirmed to her that he was as mercenary as ever. Those memories of closeness when she'd been ill must have been imagined. *They* were just a deal.

When the car pulled up at one of Rome's top hotels and she saw the throng of photographers lingering around the red carpet it made her wish she didn't have to go out there and face them all. The photographers were the least of her worries. It was the women who lived the life she was supposed to be fitting in to. Women like Capricia Conetta, who were not only past lovers of Dante's but practised in the art of snobbery. Not once had Piper felt she truly fitted in.

Dante got out of the car first, and then held her hand as she stepped onto the red carpet. The emerald-green dress showed much more of her legs than she was happy with through the long slit at the front, and she tried hard to ignore the sinfully sexy look in Dante's eyes as they filled with unconcealed desire.

It was all part of the act, she reminded herself. He was acting the role of doting fiancé. In public, nobody could question his attraction to her—nobody could doubt he wanted her—but once they were alone that act was abandoned. It was something she had to learn to do too, if she was going to survive this charade.

'Smile,' he whispered as he leant close to her—so close that when she looked up at him his lips were only a breath away from hers.

Her eyes locked with his, the rest of the world was forgotten, and all she wanted was to be kissed. All she needed was to feel his lips on hers, taste him as he pressed his body against her.

She felt her lips lift into a smile, but still she couldn't break the spell which had snared them. She heard him say something but had no idea what, or even in what language. All she could focus on was his eyes, so dark, so sexy. As his lips touched hers she closed her own eyes, unable to bear the feel of his kiss but wanting it so badly.

He didn't pull back, didn't move away, and the kiss remained light, so teasing it was pure torture. She sighed against his lips, and when he did pull back her eyes flew open. It was then she realised that the night was lit up with flashes and that all around them photographers were calling. The crowd, gathered to watch the arrival of the rich and famous, called and cheered. She blushed and swallowed hard, not knowing what to say.

'That was very convincing, *cara*.'

The mischief which sparkled in his eyes made her tingle, and excitement washed over her. She'd almost given herself away, almost let him see and feel her growing feelings for him. And that would have been the biggest mistake of all.

Finally she regained her senses. 'I thought that was what you wanted.'

Before he had a chance to respond she turned and faced the photographers, leaving him no choice but to hold her at his side. She smiled. It wasn't for her, or even for Dante. It was for her child, and for the deal she'd made with this man she'd first spent the night with because she'd wanted to prove she was alive, to prove she could feel, and most importantly could do what she wanted. How wrong it had all gone.

Moments later he led her along the red carpet and into the hotel, and momentarily she felt lost and drained of emotion. That kiss, as light as it had been, had sapped all the strength from her.

He touched the small of her back as he guided her through the already thronging party guests. Their entrance had gained the interest of some of the guests, and Piper's heart sank when she saw Capricia weaving her way through the other guests, her gaze firmly fixed on Dante.

Capricia was the last person she needed to see when she felt so fragile, so out of place in the world she'd slipped into. All day she'd fought the growing need to walk away, to forget the deal and forget Dante, but she wasn't sure she could do that. She had to think of her baby.

'*Ciao*, Dante.' Capricia all but hung on to Dante as they kissed on each cheek. 'I see you haven't tired of the protégée yet?'

Piper bit back a retort at the insult, spoken in English and clearly meant for her to understand. She didn't want to be like this woman. She remembered her childhood, standing alone at school because nobody wanted to be friends with the girl who was blind in one eye. Even then she'd had no stomach for joining in and being one of the crowd. With sinking resignation she knew she didn't belong in this world—and never would.

'Like *you* would have done?' Dante said, his voice holding a hint of flirtation. But the steely glint in his eyes gave away his true mood.

Capricia seemed oblivious to it, focusing only on the light-hearted flirtation.

'Now, if you'll excuse me, I'd like to spend time with my fiancée.'

Dante had seen the colour drain from Piper's face even before Capricia had arrived, full of gusto as usual. Dante smiled at the shock on Piper's face now, as he all but sidestepped the woman he'd had a brief affair with and took her hand, leading her through the guests.

Guilt nudged at him. He'd noticed Piper looking paler and more uncomfortable today, and had insisted on her seeing the doctor for reassurance that both mother and child were well. He didn't want to take any chances.

He felt guilty enough about pushing her into appearing with him night after night, but it had been necessary. The need to convince the world as well as Bettino D'Antonio that he had turned his back on his playboy ways and was settling down was paramount. He'd also decided to offer *Celebrity Spy!* an engagement exclusive. It would be the surest way to show as many people as possible that he was committed to his new lifestyle.

'Sorry about Capricia,' he said softly as he handed Piper a glass of water. 'That little scene is not the sort of thing that needs to be witnessed by anyone if we are to pull this deal off.'

Damn it. That wasn't what he'd meant to say. He'd wanted to tell her that she shouldn't have to listen to that—not in her condition. He'd wanted to show he cared, show he was on her side. How had it come out sounding so mercenary? So like the Dante Mancini the world thought he was?

'It just goes to prove how unbelievable it is that you have become engaged.' She didn't meet his gaze, but sipped at the water and looked around her, as if she were interested in those who had turned out for the party.

She confused him. In one moment he thought she liked all the attention, the glamorous new clothes and being part of the limelight, and then she'd say something that didn't fit in with that kind of woman.

'It's not been as easy as I had thought.' He'd spoken his mind before he'd had a chance to think again—something he never usually did...or at least he hadn't until this woman had come into his life.

'Have you heard anything from Bettino?' She glanced up at him and he couldn't miss the fierce gleam in her green eyes, making them blaze like gemstones.

He looked into the champagne which bubbled in its flute and tried to suppress the unease he felt at not having heard anything from D'Antonio yet. He'd been sure that Piper's talk of art had been enough to bring the old man round. Not yet, it appeared.

'No.' He drank down the champagne and knew he was glowering at her. He could see the uncertainty on her face. She thought he blamed *her*. Despite that thought, he couldn't temper his words. He was totally unaccustomed to not getting what he wanted in business. 'I don't understand what is taking him so long.'

'It hasn't even been a week yet since we had dinner at his villa.'

She was trying to appease him, but he could feel his temper rising.

'Too long,' he snapped, and then looked at her, trying to assess what she was going to say. Did she too think their engagement deal hadn't helped him get D'Antonio on-side?

'You could come home with me and meet my mother. If we arrived together in London that might help.'

'No.' Inwardly he cursed. Why was she so hung up on including her mother in their so-called deal? He'd explained what was what to *his* mother, who hadn't understood at all, so why did Piper need to give *her* mother a false impression of their relationship? 'I did suggest that you explain the true situation to your mother.'

He spoke quietly, but with a steely glint in his voice as he tried to keep the topic of their conversation from the other party guests. There was still a chance that his deal might come off, and just as importantly that the charity he supported would continue to want him as a patron. Helping underprivileged children realise they *did* have a value in life was something he had to do—especially after he'd been shown that one single act of kindness which had started him on his own journey of self-discovery, ultimately making him the wealthy man he now was.

'I'm only trying to help convince the media that what we have is real.'

'But it isn't, is it, *cara*?' He looked down at her, silently acknowledging that the only real thing they had was the spark of sexual attraction which had got them into this predicament in the first place and then compounded it, changing everything.

All he wanted to do now was return things to the way they'd been the morning she'd signed that contract. And if he had to push her away to make her see how unsustainable their situation was then that was what he'd do. And there was a guaranteed way to do that.

'I'd like to offer *Celebrity Spy!* an engagement exclusive.'

'What?'

Piper blinked in shock. Had she heard right? Had he actually said he'd invited the very magazine responsible for their current situation into their lives—and their lies?

'It will be the best way to show everyone we mean business.'

His dark eyes bored into hers, daring her to object, but there was no way she could do this. He'd asked too much this time, taken his need to win a business deal too far.

'*You* mean business—not me.' Disappointment

flooded her. If that didn't prove she was nothing but a business deal, even after their weekend in Tuscany, nothing would.

'You agreed to sign the contract. You even added your own terms, Piper. You can't back out now. We *will* do this interview. At least then you won't have to tire yourself by attending parties each and every night.'

Around them the hum of the party continued and Piper glanced away, looking at the women, dripping in sparkling stones and dressed in designer gowns that would probably never be worn again. She didn't belong here—at least not on this side of things. She belonged behind the scenes, in the frenzied preparations for such events.

'This isn't my world, Dante.' She could hear the resigned tone to her voice, knew that she had to find her strength if she was going to do what had to be done.

'Do you not enjoy the attention, the new clothes and the glamorous places?'

'It's not what I'm used to.'

'I find that hard to believe, *cara.*'

His voice became deep and sexy as he leant closer to her, and she knew it wasn't because he wanted to do that but because it was part of the act.

'Very well, we will leave as soon as possible.'

For the rest of the party Piper tried to ignore the icy tone of Dante's voice and his determination that their deal was as normal as any other. It wasn't for her. She'd made a deal for her child's future happiness—not a stupid business deal. And even if he did want to look better for the charity he supported it did very little to soothe the pain of his rejection. Neither did it justify appearing in a magazine posing as his fiancée.

As she stood there at the party, watching the vain and

false women, she knew that no matter what her original intentions had been she didn't want her child to grow up as a part of this life. It was a life she didn't belong to, but it was one she would have fitted into, learned to be part of, if only Dante had genuinely cared about her. He'd never love her, and their marriage would never be the fairytale she'd always dreamed of, but it could be a happy one in which to raise their child if he put aside the business deal part of their relationship.

As the hour ticked passed midnight and her energy levels dipped to an all-time low she knew it was over. She'd tried to make a go of it, tried to give Dante what he wanted, but she knew now that nothing she could do would ever be enough for him.

She wanted to leave, but the image of the contract she'd signed burned in her mind. She'd agreed to be his fiancée and then his wife for two years. Could she really endure all his world threw at her and trust that he'd keep his side of the deal?

The stark answer came back at her.

No, she couldn't.

CHAPTER TWELVE

PIPER HAD TRIED to be rational, tried to keep emotion out of her decision, but after the loneliest night of her life she finally accepted that being with Dante couldn't work. If he didn't want to commit fully to the deal they'd struck that morning in his office how would he ever be there for his child?

She'd couldn't bear the thought of her child being distraught when its father didn't show up one day, as planned, and she knew now that was exactly the kind of father Dante would be. Nothing would ever be as important as chasing the next deal. And, whilst she could never deny Dante access to his son or daughter, she wanted more for her baby. She wanted her child to have what she'd had from her father—unconditional love and a father who was there for them, no matter what.

Dante had already shown that was not how he envisaged fatherhood. The fact that he had no intention of involving his mother in their child's life left her in no doubt as to just how small a part he was prepared to play once the baby was born.

She packed the few belongings she'd arrived in Rome with into her bag and dressed in the jeans and jumper she'd worn the day she'd waited for him in his office. After a quick glance round the bedroom, which after their time in Tuscany she'd hoped he would join her in, she left, and went in search of the man she was supposed to be engaged to. Calmness had settled over her. It was over. Whatever *it* was.

'*Buongiorno.*'

He didn't even look up from the paperwork he was reading and her heart sank a little further. He had no interest in her. She was merely a pawn in his game-plan for success. He'd used her—used the fact that she'd wanted to do the right thing by him and tell him personally that their night together had resulted in a baby.

'Working so early?' She kept her voice light as she poured a glass of water and stood watching him, committing everything about the man she loved to memory.

The man she loved.

That thought stopped her, and she stood looking at him, wondering when that had happened. When had she given her heart to a man who didn't even know what emotions were, let alone love?

'I have a meeting this afternoon, and I won't be home until late this evening. So tonight you may rest. We have a dinner engagement tomorrow evening, and I will then arrange the exclusive engagement interview.'

His words, spoken so coldly, as if he was talking to an employee, broke through her startling thoughts and she looked at him. She loved this man, and she was having his baby, but it meant nothing to him.

'This isn't what I wanted, Dante.'

She said the words before she'd had a chance to think, but once they were out there, settling between them, relief filled her. She had to be true to herself and the baby. It didn't matter what she felt for Dante. Her love counted for nothing. He was unreachable, and it would break her heart to stay and try to find the man he could be—the man she wanted.

She recalled all he'd told her about Alessio. He'd had emotion then. Had the loss of his brother changed him that much?

'What isn't?' He looked at her and frowned, and the sharpness of his voice drew her thoughts back from the avenue they'd been wandering down.

He had no idea. Did he really think she wanted this lifestyle? This materialistic life where emotions were masked? Where everyone seemed to have a hidden agenda?

'The—the deal we made.' She stumbled over her words before finding an inner strength. 'It's never going to work.'

He put down the papers and came towards her, suspicion in his eyes. 'What are you suggesting?'

He was so close that if she closed her eyes and took in a deep breath she'd be able to inhale his aftershave, that fresh from the shower scent she adored so much. It reminded her of their weekend in Tuscany.

She shut her senses down, refusing to allow them to drag sentiment into her decision. Now was not the time. She had to be strong and firm—for her baby, if not herself.

She stood taller and looked into his eyes, seeing the mistrust deep within them where once she'd seen desire and passion. If they could have remained locked away in Tuscany maybe she could have got through the barriers he had around him, the impenetrable wall he used to keep people out. But as soon as he'd returned to Rome, to his sophisticated world, any genuine warmth and understanding between them had gone.

Along with his latest suggestion of an engagement

exclusive, it just added to the feeling that he'd used her—and that hurt more than anything.

'I can't be what you want.'

Those dark eyes which had once been filled with desire for her had become granite-hard, but she forced herself to say what had to be said.

'And you, Dante, can't be what I want. It won't work.'

'We made a deal.'

His eyes narrowed, but she refused to be intimidated even as he stepped closer, threatening the strength she had to hold onto.

'Yes,' she snapped, and moved back from him, needing to escape the intensity of those eyes. 'And I have tried to keep *my* side of that deal. It's not my fault Bettino hasn't gone with your company, and it certainly isn't my fault that the social circle you keep hasn't done anything more than speculate about our engagement.'

'They will speculate in an entirely different way if you revert to your usual style.'

The distaste in his eyes wasn't lost on her. He'd looked at her the same way as she'd stood before him in his office. Hurt spiked through her, reminding her of her childhood, of standing alone whilst friends whispered about her. She knew exactly why he didn't want her any more, and it had very little to do with what she chose to wear. She'd told him the truth. That she wasn't perfect. And now, because of that, she didn't fit into his world—or his plans.

'I can't be what I'm not, Dante.'

Strength she hadn't felt in days finally came to her, driving her on to do what she knew was right—even though it hurt, even though it meant turning her back on the man who'd stolen her heart. She didn't want to be that lonely child any more. Her father's love had given her the courage to accept who she was and be that person, and she needed a man like him—not one like Dante.

'Just as you can't be what I need.'

'What are you trying to say?'

The hardness in his voice almost shattered her resolve to carry through the decision she'd come to last night as she'd tossed and turned.

'I can't stay—not like this.' She spread out her palms in a gesture of hopelessness.

'What *would* you stay for? More clothes and jewels? Money?'

The ferocity of the accusation in his voice sliced at her already unbalanced emotions. He thought she was as materialistic as women like Capricia, that a shopping spree and a party would make everything right.

She gasped in shock. 'If you really think I would stay for any of that then you don't know me at all.'

Shock and disappointment were in danger of showing, so she turned from him and crossed the room, heading for the sanctuary of the bedroom. She had nothing more to say to him. She might have fallen in love with him, but if she'd had any doubts about leaving what he'd just said had confirmed it was exactly the right thing to do.

She turned and gave him one last look, and the anger in his handsome face was almost too much. 'Goodbye, Dante.'

Dante's mind reeled with shock. She was going to walk away—not only from him, but from their deal. He should be pleased. After all he had no wish to become a married man, much less a father. The thought of being responsible for someone again still filled him with pure fear. He couldn't be anyone someone needed—not when the guilt of Alessio's death still raged within him.

When Piper had told him why she'd come to Rome that guilt had deepened. She'd torn him apart, along with his life, when she'd told him she wanted something from him he just couldn't give. He wasn't capable of loving a child, of being there to see it through the trials of life, not when he'd failed his own brother so spectacularly. He couldn't do that to someone again.

'We made a deal, Piper. You signed the papers, agreed to become my wife, and that deal does not end until two years after we are married.' He forced his mind from the implications of insisting the marriage went ahead.

'What kind of marriage would it be if we continue on this disastrous course? What kind of parents will we be if this baby can't even know its grandmothers?' Piper's voice resounded with frustration.

She placed her hand over her stomach, which as yet showed no sign of the child she spoke of, but his doctor had at least confirmed she was pregnant. Should he have demanded she take the test she'd mentioned? Confirmed he was the baby's father?

Questions raced through his mind. He'd been so distracted by Piper's reappearance into his life he hadn't thought it through. Not a problem he was used to admitting. He was usually completely in control.

The last time he hadn't been in control, when he'd played the wrong cards in life, his brother had slipped away in the early-evening darkness. He'd been angry with Alessio, but even angrier with himself. Once again he'd pushed someone away by caring. He'd loved his father and he'd left them without even a goodbye. He'd loved Alessio, tried to be a father and a brother to him. All he'd wanted to do was give his brother and mother the best. But the night Alessio had left he'd closed off his heart, shut down his emotions and become the hardened man he now was. It was safer that way.

'I will not have my mother dragged into our sordid little deal.'

He knew exactly what she was doing and he wouldn't allow it. His mother had experienced enough heartache. She already blamed him for all the pain in her life, and he was damn sure Piper would not be allowed to add to her worries. All she'd ever wanted was for him to forgive himself and settle down, have children. How ironic that she would now get her wish—but he hadn't forgiven himself. That was impossible.

'You can't pretend our marriage is real—not to your mother.' The shock in her voice was clear as she stood in front of the door to his bedroom. A room he hadn't used since she'd arrived. Yet he'd slept with her in Tuscany, enjoyed the sensation of sleeping with her in his arms—something he'd never done before with any woman. Deep down he knew it had been much more than just being relaxed in the villa, that it had to do with the woman he'd held after making love to her. And it scared the hell out of him.

'I have already emailed her to explain the situation. That our engagement and subsequent marriage are for the sake of The Hope Foundation.'

He saw the pain and shock in her gorgeous eyes, saw the sparkle slip from their gemlike green, but it was the best way. It was as if he was on the brink of a crater, filled with bubbling emotion, and if he made one wrong move he'd fall in and be consumed by those emotions.

'And for your deal with Bettino.' The hurt in her

voice was plain. 'I don't believe that you can forget your deal. But what I *can* believe is that you are so cold and unfeeling you emailed your own mother with that news. How could I have ever thought that I...?'

Her words trailed off, but he didn't want to know what she'd been about to say. From the expression on her face, the worry in her eyes, he knew. How could she ever have thought she could marry him? He didn't want to hear the truth. All he wanted to do was push her further away.

Instead of thinking about the only woman who'd ever remained in his mind after a night of passion— the only woman he might have loved if things were different—instead of dwelling on that revelation, he turned his attention to his mother, and the impending meeting he had planned with her later that day.

He had been summoned to his mother's home after sending the email, but he wasn't going to admit that to Piper. He had no wish to give her such ammunition, and he certainly didn't want his mother calling at the apartment to meet Piper. He knew instinctively that if the two of them met he would lose control of everything, and control was what he sought to have at all times.

Tonight he would meet his mother and paint Piper as a woman who was as calculated and mercenary as he was. Under no circumstances would he tell her that Piper carried his child. That would give his mother too much hope, and he'd already done that to her when he'd assured her that he would find Alessio after he'd ran away. Several years later, when he *had* found him, he'd never seen such pain on his mother's face. He'd given her false hope and he wouldn't allow that to happen again.

* * *

Piper couldn't believe what she was hearing. Where had the loving man she'd spent the weekend in Tuscany with gone? This cold and mercenary man was far worse than *Celebrity Spy!* had painted him. He was everything she didn't want in a husband—or as a father for her baby.

She had no choice. She had to go. She had to leave behind her foolish dreams of happiness and return to London. She had no one else in the world but her mother, but still she didn't need such a cold-hearted man as Dante.

'How long did it take you to decide that getting engaged to me would win you your damn deal?' She hurled the words at him, icy hatred in her eyes as she watched him pick up his briefcase, put in the papers he'd been reading and click it shut.

He was going to walk out on her, leave her to fester with his rejection while he went about his day and worked into the night. He looked at her, his dark eyes assessing, and an icy chill slid over her—one that filled her with courage and determination to do what was right.

'We will talk again this evening.'

'I won't be here this evening.' She tossed the words into the charged atmosphere.

He came towards her and she stood her ground. 'You *will* be here. You signed a contract. But, more to the point, I can give you the kind of lifestyle you want.'

She walked slowly towards him, her gaze locked with his, disbelief that he could be so cold, so accusing, churning in her stomach, making her more nauseous than she'd ever been. Angrily she pushed that aside. 'I signed a contract to play the role of your fiancée in order for you to win a deal. *You* are the one who wanted to change me, turn me into someone I wasn't, someone I could never be.'

'I have not yet secured that deal.'

'You don't own me, Dante.'

Her voice quivered with passion mixed with frustration and he knew she was right.

'And I won't let you change me.'

The floodgates of emotion had opened and she couldn't hold back any longer. All the hurt and humiliation she'd bottled up rushed out before Dante could say anything.

'I can't be what you want, Dante. I'm not a puppet you can shape to fit your circumstances—and, more to the point, neither is our baby.'

'Are you trying to say you have nothing to gain from our agreed deal? What about all the clothes and jewels you have?'

'None of them matter.' Her stomach turned over again and she thought for one minute she would have to rush away to the bathroom. Would he even care?

'So what does matter, *mia cara*? What is it you really want to gain?'

There was an undertone of controlled annoyance in his tone, and she just didn't feel well enough to deal with it right now.

'If we are going to be married for the sake of the baby then I want my baby to know its grandmothers—especially as he or she won't have any grandfathers.' She stood boldly, pushing home her point, and for a moment she thought he was going to disagree, to give her a justifiable reason for not involving his or her mother in the baby's life.

'I can't have this conversation—not now, not ever.'

He put on his jacket and picked up his briefcase. 'We made a deal. Let's just stick to it, no?'

'No,' she said firmly, and saw his eyes widen in surprise. Had nobody ever said no to the all-powerful Dante Mancini?

He marched to the door, yanked it open and turned to face her. 'We made a deal, Piper, and nothing changes—not a thing. But right now I'm late.'

'Just go, Dante. I never want to see you again. I made a big mistake coming here—one I intend to rectify.'

CHAPTER THIRTEEN

DANTE LOOKED BRIEFLY at his phone as Bettino D'Antonio disconnected the call. He should be punching the air for joy. He'd got the contract, but somehow with Piper gone he didn't care. None of it mattered if he didn't have her to share it with. His elation at having secured his most lucrative deal yet was swamped by misgivings.

He cursed under his breath and slid his phone back into his jacket pocket.

'Problems?' His mother's question couldn't quite drag him from the low he'd been in since he'd arrived back at his apartment two days ago to find Piper had actually gone against their contract and left. Just as she'd told him she would.

She'd taken nothing other than what she'd arrived with—not even the engagement ring she'd selected. She'd left it on his desk, next to her copy of the contract, making it clear what she thought of both. He'd never felt more adrift in life as he did now.

'No.' He tried for an enthusiastic approach, but fell way short of it if the expression on his mother's face was anything to go by. 'That was about the deal I've been chasing. I've got it. I now own one of the biggest solar energy companies.'

His mother frowned and for a moment he saw Alessio in the reproach that filled her eyes. He'd always thought Alessio took after their mother. They had the same nutmeg eyes, and she would often look at him the way his younger brother had. It was another constant reminder of his guilt, as if Alessio was still there, reprimanding him for not looking after him.

'Was the deal worth it?'

'Of course.' He tried not to think about the deal he'd made with Piper, the deal for his child, just to secure a contract to make his renewable energies company one of the biggest in the world.

'Are you certain about that?'

What was his mother trying to do? Make him feel even worse than he already did?

Stifled by emotions he just couldn't analyse now, he grabbed his car keys. 'I need to get back to Rome—put things in motion with D'Antonio.'

'You need to go to London first.'

His mother's voice was gentle, as always, but beneath that softness he heard steely determination.

'You have things to sort out there, Dante.'

It was as if he'd slammed into a wall, and exactly the reason he'd wanted to keep Piper and his mother apart. His mother had never met her, didn't know about the baby, but already she was on Piper's side. Even though he'd explained about the cold and calculated deal Piper had agreed to—leaving out one important detail—his mother was looking for more. What *was* it with women wanting happy-ever-afters that could never exist?

'I will not be chasing after *that* particular contract. It has fallen through, but at least it appears to have achieved what I wanted.' As he finished speaking he gritted his teeth against his anger that Piper had walked out on him—again. Anger that was mixed with hurt. He missed her. He wanted her. In a way he'd never thought possible. And she'd walked away.

'Is a contract for a solar energy company worth more than your happiness?' his mother asked quietly, but the firmness of the question let him know just what she thought of that. She'd always told him he worked too hard.

He was proud of his company, but he never stopped working—never stopped making it bigger and better, as if he was still searching for something to make things right. Because so far nothing was right. Why should now be any different from when his father had left or Alessio had gone missing? He was getting what he deserved once more. He'd messed up again. He'd driven Piper away, and with her his child.

'Business is my happiness. Now I have to go.'

He couldn't discuss this now. Not when he knew his mother spoke the truth. A truth he wasn't yet ready to admit.

Dante turned to go.

'You have to stop punishing yourself, Dante. Alessio's death wasn't your fault.'

His mother's words made another step too difficult. His mind raced back in time to the day he'd last seen his father and the words he'd said before he left. *'Look after them.'*

It might have been just something to say for a man so selfish he had walked out on his young family but Dante, at almost eight, had assumed the role of protector and, even before he'd finished school, provider. His need to succeed had come from that moment.

'You were a child when your father left...'

His mother's words snagged his attention and he

turned to look at her, unaware that he was clenching his fists so tightly the car keys dug into his palm.

'I never wanted you to take his place. I wanted you to be a child, to grow up in your own time.'

'I couldn't watch you struggle.' He growled the words as pain engulfed him. 'He left me in charge. He made me the man of the house when I was still a boy.'

'And I blame myself for what it's done to you.'

The raw emotion in his mother's voice only intensified the anger he felt towards his father and his guilt at letting Alessio down.

'You shouldn't shut love out of your life, Dante. Live for yourself—not your father.'

As the words sluiced round in his mind images of Piper—of her smile as they'd enjoyed their time in Tuscany, of the passion in her eyes as he'd made her his once more and the pain in her voice as she'd told him she couldn't do it any more—collided with the past. Had love played any part in that for her?

'I don't need love.'

He'd spoken more to himself than his mother, but as the harsh words left him he knew it was a lie. With Piper he'd seen what love and happiness could be like, had glimpsed a life he had no right to want.

'I've seen the photos, Dante, and the television coverage. That woman loves you.'

'No,' he snapped quickly. 'It's all part of the deal to make the world think we are in love.'

'Just as you love her.' She walked towards him, her eyes pleading with him. 'Go to her, Dante, and make this right—for you and for her, but most of all for the baby.'

The air around him snapped, and shock snatched his ability to speak. How did his mother know what he'd tried so hard to keep from her? *Maledizione.* He'd only told Elizabeth Young out of necessity.

'I'm right, aren't I? A woman knows these things.'

He knew then it was pointless denying anything.

'About the baby? Yes.' Resignation filled him. The one thing he hadn't wanted to do was give his mother hope of being a grandmother, hope that he'd settle down and have a family. He'd never wanted that—until he'd met Piper. Now he would have to break his mother's heart too.

'No, I'm right that you love her.'

The insistent tone wrenched him from his despondent thoughts. 'You've got it wrong.' He flung the words at his mother as he left her villa, needing the solitude of his car and the drive back to Rome.

He needed to think, to process everything, to sort his emotions out—emotions he'd banished from his life years ago. Emotions he shouldn't want, but did. So why did he want them back now?

He was in love with Piper.

Piper's morning sickness had become much worse since her arrival back in London. She had spilled the whole story to her mother, who'd held her as she'd cried. As the tears had dried Piper had felt guilty, sure her mother would blame herself for dragging her away from Sydney and all she'd grown up with.

Her friends, Katie and Jo, had rallied round with emails and calls, giving her support, but there wasn't much else they could do so far away in Sydney, and Piper had never felt so alone. She wished her father was there to tell her it would be all right in the end. She could almost hear him now. *'There's a happy-ever-after out there for you, Piper, don't ever forget that.'*

He'd said it many times to her as she'd grown up, and she'd always teased him about it, but right now a happy-ever-after with Dante was all she wanted. But that was a futile wish, and leaving Rome—leaving the man she loved—certainly hadn't felt right.

For the first few days in London Piper had been angry with Dante, but now she had reached a stage of acceptance. The man she loved didn't and couldn't love her. It had been four days since she'd left Rome and she'd heard nothing from him. She didn't even know if he'd got his deal with Bettino D'Antonio. All she knew was that her heart was breaking and she didn't know how to mend it.

A firm knock on the front door of the house her mother rented startled her from her misery and a little light of hope sparked in her heart. Had he come for her? Then it faded as quickly as it had flared. Dante wouldn't come after her—not when he was incapable of any kind of emotion. He wouldn't let it into his life. He was completely closed off to it. He'd probably already moved on to the next woman in his life, while she would remain in love with him for ever, with their child a legacy and constant reminder of him.

With a heavy heart she opened the door, the blast of cold from England's winter weather momentarily taking her breath away. Then she saw Dante, and her knees weakened and her stomach somersaulted.

He looked devastatingly handsome. The warm coat he wore over his suit gave him an air of distinction, and she remembered how she'd thought the same that night of the party. The night he'd kissed her, right there in front of everyone, as they'd stood on the red carpet, cameras flashing, recording the moment. That kiss had been so full of passion and desire, as if he'd really meant it, had really wanted to kiss her. It had given her hope—but false hope, and she'd had to accept it was all part of the act.

'Piper?'

The question in his voice as he said her name unsettled her nerves, and the firm and determined expression on his face warned her not to expect things she knew he couldn't give. Not when she'd run out on their deal.

She'd had to leave. For her sanity. Each day her love had grown, and the pain of knowing he'd never love her had increased until it had become unbearable.

'What do you want, Dante? I thought we'd said all we needed to say.' She folded her arms and stood on the doorstep, the partially open door behind her. All she wanted to do was protect herself, hide her love, her elation at seeing him, but the embers of something dark smouldered in his eyes, increasing her nerves tenfold.

'We have things to settle—about the baby.'

He took a step towards her and instinctively she held her ground. She couldn't let him over the threshold of her new life. It was still such a painful choice, and she was scared he'd make her fragile strength evaporate, make her change her mind.

'I suggest we leave all that to the legal experts.'

She wasn't going to force him to be a father, to be part of her baby's life, and she certainly wasn't going to sort out the final details with him now. She'd taken her mother's advice and arranged to seek legal help, determined to find a way out of their contract.

'Is that what you want?'

His voice was icy-cold, his eyes so dark she couldn't decipher what emotion was in them.

'I didn't want *any* of this.'

The pain of it all—of holding back her emotions—made those words a strangled cry and she turned, fleeing into the house. She heard the front door close behind her, heard the noise of the street subside, and knew there was no getting away from him. She stood in the living room of the small terraced house, looking at her reflection in the mirror above the fireplace, wondering how her life had become so wildly complicated.

Because you love him.

The words rushed around her mind. When had it happened? *How* had she fallen in love with a man such as Dante? She didn't really need to ask those silent questions. She already knew. She'd fallen in love with him the night they'd first met—the night he'd made her his for evermore.

As she looked into the mirror Dante entered the small room, his gaze meeting hers, and the intensity of it sent a shiver of awareness all over her. For a moment she wished he loved her too, that he was here because he couldn't imagine life without her in it.

'What was it you came to Rome for?'

Dante's question was fired at her, but she held his gaze in the mirror, trying to read those dark eyes which hid every hint of emotion.

Finally she turned to face him, but the firm set of his jaw, shadowed with stubble as it had been that first morning in Rome, made her nerves desert her.

'We've gone over this, Dante. All I wanted to do was let you know you were going to be a father. Nothing more. You were the one who turned it all into something else. You made it into a deal—something sordid and soul-destroying—just to win a business deal.'

'Then why did you sign the contract?'

His accent had become more pronounced and that

shiver of awareness notched up a level. How could he affect her so much after all he'd done?

'I wanted my baby to have what *I* had—a father who cared, one who would spend time with it, and most importantly one who would be there, no matter what. But you can't be that—can you, Dante?'

She knew she was pushing him, forcing him to face all he'd hidden from since Alessio's death. But what else did she have to lose? *Nothing*.

A flicker of pain crossed his face, showing itself in the darkness of his eyes so very briefly she wondered if she'd imagined it.

'No, I can't be that man.'

His abrupt admission sliced at her heart and she closed her eyes against the raw emotion in his voice.

'That man isn't inside me, Piper. I can't be what you need.'

Her eyes flew open and she saw he stood closer to her now...so close that if she chose to she could step into his embrace. But would that make things right?

'Just as I can't be the woman you need, Dante. But I *could* live in your world, be all the things you need, if only...'

Her words faltered and she lowered her gaze, unable to look into those eyes any longer. How had she been so stupid? She'd nearly admitted that his love was all she needed to make everything right. That if she could love him too then nothing else would matter.

'If only what, Piper?'

He stepped closer and reached out, pushed her hair from her face so gently she was sure he had been anxious about startling her. She looked up at him, shyness engulfing her at the sight of the desire which burned in his eyes. But she wouldn't be swayed by lust—not again.

'It doesn't matter,' she said slowly, and stepped away from him, not able to bear being so close without being in his arms. 'I guess if you'd got the deal it would have been worth it.'

'I did get the deal.'

Dante had to clench his hands in an attempt not to reach for her again, not to touch the softness of her flame hair, or feel the warmth of her skin. Everything she'd said suggested their deal had been all about mutually beneficial arrangements, that every moment they'd shared in Tuscany had been just part of the deal.

He was shocked at how much it mattered, but it did. As he'd sat on the flight to London he'd played his mother's words over and over in his mind. Each word had confirmed what he'd known all along, what he'd been running from since he'd seen her again in his office. He wanted Piper. He loved her. And that terrified him.

'So everything you set out to achieve has happened?'

She prickled with indignation and injustice, and he'd done that to her.

'*Sì*, it has—but I still have my part of our deal to keep.' He watched her pretty face frown in disbelief at his words, and knew if he'd been on the receiving end of the way he'd treated her he wouldn't trust a word he said.

'I don't expect anything from you, Dante. In fact I don't want anything except for you to go back to your life and let me live mine. Go, Dante—just go.'

How could he go back to his life and leave her here? 'No, that's not possible.'

She glared at him, the angry sparkle in her eyes, reminding him of fireworks. For the second time in his life he was far from in control of a situation. The fear that had swamped him when Alessio had left was nothing compared to the way he felt right now.

'No, I'm not going back—not until I've made things right with you.'

'Right? Nothing can ever be right now.'

Her eyes glittered with unshed tears. He was hurting her, but he had to say what he needed to—no matter how hard it was going to be.

'I want us to be married, as planned.'

'Are you *insane*?' Her voice rose as she spoke, her eyes wide in shock. 'I can't live a lie like that.'

'Just as I can't.'

'Your whole life is a lie, Dante, so why have you developed a conscience suddenly?'

'Because I was wrong.' Nerves made the admission almost stick in his throat, but he forced himself on. 'Because I love you.'

Silence fell over the room. Like a sheer veil, it doused all the angry tension. Piper stood in the middle of the room, so very close he could reach out and touch her, but she felt further away than she'd ever done.

'You don't mean that.' The whispered words slipped from her as she searched his face, looking for evidence of lies or truth.

Finally he moved towards her. He had to tell her now exactly how he felt or lose her for ever. 'What we have—'

'Is just lust.'

She cut across his words, savaging his attempt to tell her he couldn't live without her. But he hadn't got where he was in life by admitting defeat, so easily.

'At first it was,' he admitted, lifting his hands quickly in frustration and walking away from her to stand at the large bay window which looked out onto the street.

He turned back to her. 'But that has changed. I don't know when it happened, or how, but I love you, Piper.'

He reached into his pocket and retrieved the engagement ring he'd bought her in Rome.

'I don't believe you.'

His heart sank. She didn't want him—didn't want to listen to him, to hear how much he loved her. 'Then there is nothing more to say, except that you are the woman who changed me, who made me see life again as it should be and taught me that I can love someone— and that someone is you.'

'What about the deal?' she asked cautiously. 'Is that why you still want us to marry?'

'The only deal I want from you is one secured by two words at the altar.' He held the ring up between his thumb and finger. 'I want you to wear my ring— for real.'

She moved towards him and he waited, hoping, needing her to come freely to him so he could hold her and kiss her, knowing she was his.

'Is that a proposal?'

She smiled, and her teasing words brought relief and a smile to his own lips. There was hope.

'*Sì, mia cara. Vuoi sparsami?*'

She frowned at him, then whispered, 'Say it again in English.'

'My darling, will you marry me?'

To his relief she flung her arms around his neck and as she kissed his face, his lips, gave him her reply. 'Yes—yes, of course I will. I love you, Dante.'

He took her face between his hands and looked into those green eyes. 'And I love *you*—for ever.'

EPILOGUE

PIPER STOOD OUTSIDE the church as the hot sun of summer beat down. Her best friends, Katie and Jo from Sydney, were taking their roles as bridesmaids very seriously and fussed around her, straightening the long cream lace gown she and Elizabeth had selected as a wedding dress soon after Mia had been born.

'You look gorgeous. You are positively glowing,' Katie said as she stood back, and Piper knew it was love that shone from her.

'Not as gorgeous as this little one,' Jo added as she handed Piper the most precious addition to her bridal outfit.

Baby Mia was wearing a pale pink dress, the same shade as Katie and Jo's, with an amazingly intricate and delicate mini-bouquet of wild flowers trailing from her.

'Here she is. Your little flower girl.'

'I'm so happy,' Piper said as she looked at her friends.

Mia gave a little moan of protest at being moved, but quickly settled into her arms. Piper still couldn't believe the perfect little bundle was hers, or that life could be so good.

After she'd returned to Rome with Dante her life had changed, becoming the loving fairytale she'd always longed for. Even fitting in with Rome's social circle had been easier with Dante's love. Now she was about to top it all and become his wife.

'So what are you waiting for? Go in there and marry the man of your dreams.'

Katie grinned at her and Piper's heart fluttered along with the butterflies in her stomach.

As she left the sunshine for the cool and dark interior of the old church she saw Dante standing with his back to her and her heart went out to him. She knew even after all his admissions that this would be hard for him without Alessio, just as it was hard for her without her father, but together they'd heal each other.

She walked towards Dante, admiring him as he turned to look at her, his handsome face full of a happiness which matched hers. His dark suit fitted him perfectly, showcasing the toned and delicious body she knew so well.

With each step she moved nearer to him, nearer to being his wife, she passed their friends, flown in to the small Tuscan village from all over the world, and then their mothers, and she smiled, pleased they had found a new friendship in each other, and that her mother had made the move to Italy to be close to her new granddaughter. Each mother had known hard times, but each of them had recognised the love between her and Dante long before they themselves had.

Piper had worried that walking up the aisle alone would be hard, but as her father's words played again in her mind, she knew he'd been right all along. Dante was the happy-ever-after which had been out there for her, and she'd found him because of her father. If she hadn't been so upset that night she would never have left the dinner party with Dante.

Just before the flower-decorated altar Bettino

D'Antonio waited for her, ready to step into his role of giving her away.

Then Dante turned to her and his smile was full of love, his eyes full of warmth, and it felt like coming home. 'You look beautiful.'

A warm glow filled her at his words, and then he touched his daughter's face and took her hand.

'Let's get married.'

As words of Italian and English flowed around them, binding them together in marriage, she could hardly take her eyes from this man she loved with all her heart.

'I love you, Piper Mancini,' Dante said as he brushed his lips lightly over hers.

'And I love *you*, my darling husband.' Piper smiled at him, then looked down at her baby daughter—the most perfect wedding gift.

'I'm so very happy,' he whispered as he looked into her eyes. 'And so in love with my beautiful wife and gorgeous daughter.'

Before she could say anything he kissed her again, so very gently, yet so wickedly full of desire she thought she might dissolve right there.

'Come. It is time to start our new life,' he said as he put his arm around her and led her back down the aisle and towards the sunshine, passing friends, family and—more significantly—other soon-to-be reformed bachelors.

* * * * *

The BRIDES FOR BILLIONAIRES *series*
continues with
MARRIED FOR THE SHEIKH'S DUTY
by Tara Pammi
Available December 2016

In the meantime, if you enjoyed this story,
check out these other great reads
from Rachael Thomas
TO BLACKMAIL A DI SIONE
THE SHEIKH'S LAST MISTRESS
NEW YEAR AT THE BOSS'S BIDDING
FROM ONE NIGHT TO WIFE
Available now!

MILLS & BOON®

MODERN™

POWER, PASSION AND IRRESISTIBLE TEMPTATION

A sneak peek at next month's titles...

In stores from 17th November 2016:

- **A Di Sione for the Greek's Pleasure** – Kate Hewitt
- **The Greek's Christmas Bride** – Lynne Graham
- **A Royal Vow of Convenience** – Sharon Kendrick
- **Married for the Sheikh's Duty** – Tara Pammi

In stores from 1st December 2016:

- **The Prince's Pregnant Mistress** – Maisey Yates
- **The Guardian's Virgin Ward** – Caitlin Crews
- **The Desert King's Secret Heir** – Annie West
- **Surrendering to the Vengeful Italian** – Angela Bissell

Just can't wait?
Buy our books online a month before they hit the shops!
www.millsandboon.co.uk

Also available as eBooks.

6/01

MILLS & BOON®

EXCLUSIVE EXTRACT

Natalia Di Sione hasn't left the family estate in years, but she must retrieve her grandfather's lost book of poems from Angelos Menas! The lives of the brooding Greek and his daughter were changed irrevocably by a fire, and Talia finds herself drawn to the formidable tycoon. She knows the untold pleasure Angelos offers is limited, but when she leaves with the book, will her heart remain behind on the island?

Read on for a sneak preview of
A DI SIONE FOR THE GREEK'S PLEASURE
by Kate Hewitt

"Talia…" Angelos's voice broke on her name, and then, before she could even process what was happening, he pulled her towards him, his hands hard on her shoulders as his mouth crashed down on hers and plundered its soft depths.

It had been ten years since she'd been kissed, and then only a schoolboy's brush. She'd never been kissed like this, never felt every sense blaze to life, every nerve ending tingle with awareness, nearly painful in its intensity, as Angelos's mouth moved on hers and he pulled her tightly to him.

His hard contours collided against her softness, each point of contact creating an unbearably exquisite ache of longing as she tangled her hands in his hair and fit her mouth against his.

She was a clumsy, inexpert kisser, not sure what to do with her lips or tongue, only knowing that she wanted more of this. Of him.

She felt his hand slide down to cup her breast, his palm

hot and hard through the thin material of her dress, and a gasp of surprise and delight escaped her.

That small sound of pleasure was enough to jolt Angelos out of his passion-fogged daze, for he dropped his hand and in one awful, abrupt movement tore his mouth from hers and stepped back.

"I'm sorry," he said, his voice coming out in a ragged gasp.

"No…" Talia pressed one shaky hand to her buzzing lips as she tried to blink the world back into focus. "Don't be sorry," she whispered. "It was wonderful."

"I shouldn't have—"

"Why not?" she challenged. She felt frantic with the desperate need to feel and taste him again, and more importantly, not to have him withdraw from her, not just physically, but emotionally. Angelos didn't answer and she forced herself to ask the question again. "Why not, Angelos?"

"Because you are my employee, and I was taking advantage of you," he gritted out. "It was not appropriate…"

"I don't care about appropriate," she cried. She knew she sounded desperate and even pathetic but she didn't care. She wanted him. She *needed* him. "I care about you," she confessed, her voice dropping to a choked whisper, and surprise and something worse flashed across Angelos's face. He shook his head, the movement almost violent and terribly final.

"No, Talia," he told her flatly. "You don't."

Don't miss
A DI SIONE FOR THE GREEK'S PLEASURE
by Kate Hewitt

Available December 2016

www.millsandboon.co.uk
Copyright ©2016 Harlequin Books S.A.

Give a 12 month subscription to a friend today!

Call Customer Services
0844 844 1358[*]

or visit
millsandboon.co.uk/subscription

* This call will cost you 7 pence per minute plus your phone company's price per minute access charge.

MILLS & BOON®

Why shop at millsandboon.co.uk?

Each year, thousands of romance readers find their perfect read at millsandboon.co.uk. That's because we're passionate about bringing you the very best romantic fiction. Here are some of the advantages of shopping at www.millsandboon.co.uk:

* **Get new books first**—you'll be able to buy your favourite books one month before they hit the shops

* **Get exclusive discounts**—you'll also be able to buy our specially created monthly collections, with up to 50% off the RRP

* **Find your favourite authors**—latest news, interviews and new releases for all your favourite authors and series on our website, plus ideas for what to try next

* **Join in**—once you've bought your favourite books, don't forget to register with us to rate, review and join in the discussions

Visit **www.millsandboon.co.uk**
for all this and more today!

ILLS_WEB